Horse of Fire

Patricia Leitch started riding when a friend persuaded her to go on a pony trekking holiday – and by the following summer she had her own Highland pony, Kirsty. She wrote her first book shortly after this and writing is now her full-time occupation, but she has also done all sorts of different jobs, including being a riding-school instructor, groom, teacher and librarian. She lives in Renfrewshire, Scotland, with a bearded collie called Meg.

Patricia Leitch

Horse of Fire

An Original Armada

Horse of Fire was first published in Armada in 1986
Second impression 1988

Armada is an imprint of the
Children's Division, part of
the Collins Publishing Group,
8 Grafton Street, London W1X 3LA

Copyright © Patricia Leitch 1986

Printed and bound in Great Britain by
William Collins Sons & Co. Ltd, Glasgow

CHAPTER ONE

Jinny Manders sat in the hall of Inverburgh Comprehensive School and galloped Shantih, her chestnut Arabian mare, over the bleak Finmory moors.

Deaf to the clatter of chairs, the stamping of feet, children's voices and teachers' shouting. Jinny heard only the whine of wind through ruined bracken and bleached bones of heather, the sharp clip as Shantih's galloping hooves struck sudden outcrops of rock. She saw only the far-reaching curves of moorland, the bulk of dark mountains compacted beneath the metal weight of the sky and far below her the tooled, pewter sea. Through this drear landscape Shantih soared over stone walls and stretched out in an ecstacy of flying speed, while Jinny sat neat and tight, balanced over her horse's withers, her own red-gold hair bannering behind her as she urged her horse to greater speed.

'You asleep?' asked the girl sitting next to Jinny as she dug her elbow into Jinny's arm. 'That girl over there is trying to speak to you.'

Jinny jerked back to present reality, was aware of the school hall rapidly filling with pupils and the empty chairs marshalled on the stage waiting for the headmaster, Minister and guests. In another two hours the school Christmas service would be over and the holidays would have begun. Days of freedom, freedom to ride Shantih lay ahead of her.

'Over there,' said the girl, pointing to the other side of the hall.

Somehow Jinny had got separated from the rest of her

form and was sitting with children from another second year class. She stretched forward until she could see her form mates. Dolina Thomson who came from Ardtallon, the next village to Glenbost which was the village closest to Finmory House, was waving furiously at her.

'I have to be seeing you,' Dolina mouthed across at Jinny. 'Urgent it is.'

'What?' Jinny demanded, trying to keep her voice lower than the noise in the hall, yet loud enough to reach Dolina. 'What is it?'

'Urgent message from . . . .' Dolina shouted back as a teacher's hand closed on her shoulder, dragging her from her seat and forcing her to stand at the back of the hall.

Jinny watched helplessly. Normally she saw her on the school bus but this morning Dolina's father had been coming in to the market and had given Dolina a lift. Jinny couldn't imagine what urgent message she could have for her. It wasn't even as if Dolina was horsy, so it couldn't be anything about Shantih, and if it wasn't about Shantih Jinny didn't think it was likely to be too urgent.

The teachers' macaw voices screeched for silence and the headmaster led the platform-sitters into the hall.

'Two hours more,' thought Jinny and let herself slip back into her daydream. She felt the gentle touch of Shantih's mouth against the bit and the thrust of her powerful muscles. The headmaster's black-gowned figure vanished from sight.

'That's you, isn't it?' said the girl next to Jinny. 'Don't tell me you're asleep again?'

'Special Art prize, Jennifer Manders.'

Stumbling to her feet, Jinny knew from the tone of the headmaster's voice that this wasn't the first time he had called her name. Never before had Jinny won a school prize. Normally she was near the bottom of her form, thinking all lessons except Art and some English so boring

6

that she had dreamt and drawn her way through them until this term, when permission to show jump Shantih had depended on how well she did in the exams. She had been sixth in her form, but the thought of any prize never entered Jinny's head.

She nearly tripped hurrying up the steps to the platform, aware of giggling frothing over the hall as she stood staring at the double row of seated zombies. At the far end of the platform a ferret-sharp woman was standing by a table holding a book in Jinny's direction. Her pink lips lifted from brilliantly white teeth as she smiled coldly at Jinny, who hurried across to her, grabbed the book in her right hand and looked stupidly at the woman's outstretched hand.

'Can't shake hands,' thought Jinny, watching her own idiocy from high above her head. 'I'm holding a book. . .'

'The other hand, dear,' said the woman and in changing her prize to her left hand, Jinny dropped it. She dived under the table to retrieve it and banged her head on the table. To the roars and cheers of the school Jinny had her hand squeezed by the ferret and fled the platform, hot-cheeked with shame.

'For goodness sake, sit there,' said a not-amused teacher's voice and thankfully Jinny collapsed into a vacant seat in the second row.

'Not my fault,' she thought. 'All the rest practised that hand shaking bit. They knew they were going to get a prize but I bloomin' didn't.'

Then for the first time she looked at it. It was a book of John Skeaping's horse drawings. Turning the pages Jinny was lost in delight. With a few sure lines the artist had created racehorses, polo ponies and wild, galloping horses. They came leaping, alive, from the pages of the book.

'At this Christmas in the twentieth century, I ask myself

how the three Kings would have travelled to worship the child. The traditional camels seem unlikely. High tech suggests Concorde or space shuttle. You will each have your own ideas,' preached the headmaster's voice.

Suddenly Jinny was listening to him. She knew exactly how she would travel to find the Christ Child, for of course, she would ride Shantih. Golden, galloping, enchanted, Shantih would carry her to the stable where Jesus lay.

'However you travel,' continued the headmaster, 'I would like you to consider what gifts you would bring with you. Frankincense, or Frankenstein as my five year old daughter would have it, and myrrh are more than a little remote to our way of life. Maybe a computer would be more appropriate. A painting by Francis Bacon or a nuclear warhead? A football scarf or roller boots? A television set perhaps? Yet I think that today's Christ might be hoping for more than material gifts, would find most acceptable the gift of an awakened consciousness.

'Each one of us has many things in our lives that we do not care to look at too closely or think about too much. Perhaps our gift to the Child this Christmas might be to look at one of these hidden corners in our minds, to really look at it, and when we have acknowledged the reality of starving children in a world of plenty, or the way we treat our gran, or the time we waste staring at TV soaps, see if there is something we can do about it, now we know.

'Still, I have kept you here long enough. A very happy Christmas holiday to you all,' and his open armed gesture released his school.

Pushing her way to the cloakroom, Jinny was looking out for Dolina but could see no sign of her.

'Urgent? What could be urgent?' Jinny's brain computed possibilities.

'Congratulations,' said her Art teacher's voice.

8

'Super book,' grinned Jinny.

'Thought you'd like it. Jinny Skeaping someday?' he added as the press of children carried him on past Jinny.

'A book for the Child,' Jinny thought, 'A book of my drawings and paintings of Shantih?' But Jinny knew that the headmaster would not consider a few paintings enough. To try to stop fighting with Petra her sixteen year old, pluperfect sister who was two years older than Jinny and was always, always right? That would be more the kind of thing he had in mind.

There was no sign of Dolina in the cloakroom nor was she on the school bus that took them to Glenbost.

'Need to phone her,' thought Jinny. 'Can't wait until I bump into her in Mrs Simpson's shop.'

At Glenbost village, Jinny and Mike, her eleven year old brother who had only started at Inverburgh Comprehensive that year, jumped off the bus and into the bitter wind.

'Freedom,' said Jinny swinging her arms, long hair and school bag in delirious circles. 'I'm going to do nothing but ride Shantih!'

'Surprise, surprise,' said Mike as they hurried over to the field where Shantih and Bramble, the black Highland who was on loan from Miss Tuke's trekking centre, waited for them.

'Dolina was looking for you,' remembered Mike, vaulting over the field gate. 'Knickers in a twist, whatever it is she wants to tell you. Her dad took her off in his car. Wouldn't wait.'

Jinny flung her arms round Shantih's neck, burying her face in the silken mane and breathing in the warm, pungent smell of Arab horse.

'Dear horse,' she murmured. 'Your last day for ages, hanging round this field waiting for me to come home from school,' and Jinny gave Shantih a secret sugar lump.

With a pig squeal of jealousy, Bramble came barging up, knocking Mike to the ground.

For a moment there was a panic of splurging horses and plunging hooves as Mike struggled to find his feet and Jinny shouted at Bramble, her voice shrill with disaster.

'Your bloomin' fault,' said Mike emerging unharmed. 'I could have been kicked to death. You know you can't feed Shantih titbits. Bramble always smells them.'

'Sorry,' said Jinny contritely. 'I forgot.'

She dragged off Shantih's New Zealand rug, fetched her tack from the shed and with numbed fingers struggled to fasten throat-lash and girths.

In minutes they were both mounted and, riding through the gateway, they turned their horses into the wind, to ride the moorland road from Glenbost to Finmory.

Over two years ago the Manders family had come to live in the north of Scotland, leaving their Stopton city flat for Finmory House, a stone built house that stood four square with moorlands and mountains behind it and Finmory bay in front of it. Mr Manders had left his job as a probation officer and become a potter and author, writing books about the appalling conditions in the Stopton slums where he had worked.

Neck arched, Shantih fought against the bit, seeing no reason why she shouldn't gallop for home, while Bramble crabbed sullenly along, his head turned against the wind, ignoring the staccato beat of Mike's heels.

'I won a prize,' Jinny shouted back, seeing Mike hadn't mentioned it.

'Made a right fool of yourself!'

Jinny groaned. When Petra won prizes or passed piano exams everyone was full of praise for her, but Jinny's first, and possibly last prize, was going to be something to laugh about. Jinny eased her fingers on Shantih's reins and the Arab surged forward at an extended trot. Hearing

Bramble's hoofbeats clattering up behind her Jinny guided Shantih onto the edge of the short, moorland grass and Shantih changed into her floating canter. Jinny knew that Bramble could never keep up with her. If Mike wanted to tease her she didn't have to listen to him.

Although it was only early afternoon the moors and mountains were veiled in grey, not mist but a grey shrouding that leeched all colour from the land. Jinny rode through an etched world where even the bitter ice wind was mineral. But the weather made no difference – enamelled blue-green of summer, sheeting rain on the fire colours of autumn or this grey, moon landscape, Jinny loved it always. She never wanted to live anywhere else.

'Christmas,' Jinny thought, letting the night-light anticipation of Christmas begin to glow in her head.

Suddenly Shantih flung herself into the middle of the road, stopped dead and with a half rear stood splay-legged to face the moorland, her giraffe neck holding her head high.

'Prime time idiot,' Jinny ranted, pushing herself back into the saddle. 'What did you see?'

As if in answer to her question Shantih sent a trumpeting whinny over the moor and waited with prick-eared intensity for a reply.

'You nearly had it that time,' said Mike cheerfully, catching up. 'Thought you were off. Serve you right for bashing on.'

'What was it?'

'Look, can't you see them?'

Jinny screwed up her eyes, stared into the grey blindness and realised that the hillside was alive with red deer bolting out of sight. In the camouflage of the moor only their white rumps gave them away.

'Never seen them ɔ low down and masses of them,' she exclaimed.

'Going to be bad weather,' said Mike.

'All the same,' insisted Jinny. 'They don't usually come down so far.'

'Perhaps Mr MacKenzie is going to start farming them and Betsy's been rounding them up for him.'

'Yuch!' said Jinny in disgust, remembering the time she had gone to the Highland Show with her school and seen domesticated red deer being fed titbits by children, while next to their enclosure a marquee advertised veniburgers for sale. 'Yuch and double!'

Some of the hinds had stopped on a crest of moorland, heads raised, breathing-in the wind, making even Shantih seem a heavy, cold-blooded creature.

'Come on. I'm freezing,' said Jinny quickly and gathering Shantih together she trotted on, away from the thought of the enclosed deer.

'Might as well pick up the milk,' said Mike as Mr MacKenzie's farm, the only other dwelling near Finmory, came into sight.

'Oke,' agreed Jinny and when she reached the farm she rode Shantih into the yard.

Mr MacKenzie, hearing the horses' hooves, emerged from the barn.

'It is your father was for collecting the milk this morning,' he told them, his words escaping from the crack between his upturned collar and the peak of his tweed cap pulled down over his ears. 'I'm thinking it is the ice age that is at us.'

'Couldn't get at you,' said Jinny looking down at the huddled caddis shell of the old farmer. His ancient coat was tied around with binder twine and reached from his nose to his tacketty boots. Its long sleeves covered his hands.

'That it will not. It is the long johns I have on and yourselves could be doing with the same.'

'The deer could do with them,' said Mike. 'They've come right down from the hills.'

'Aye, they have.'

'It's the cold that brings them down?' asked Mike.

'You could be saying so. It's uneasy they are. Did you set eyes on the white one?'

'You mean the white stag they talk about?' said Jinny. Every winter someone mentioned the white stag, saying that some farmer on an outlying croft had caught a glimpse of it, but despite all her moorland riding Jinny had never seen the white stag. She didn't really believe it existed. Perhaps once there had been a white stag but not now. Not a real white stag.

'That's only a story,' she said.

'You are saying so,' replied Mr MacKenzie, his washed blue eyes gimleting up at Jinny from underneath his cap.

'I'll be over tomorrow morning,' said Mike riding Bramble out of the yard. During his holidays Mike spent most of his time at the farm.

'That will be fine,' said Mr MacKenzie without lifting his gaze from Jinny's face.

'Bye,' said Jinny. For no reason she felt suddenly awkward. She wanted to escape from Mr MacKenzie, to be back at home telling her parents about her prize.

'Be listening to me for a moment,' Mr MacKenzie said holding onto Shantih's rein. 'Some would say it was the cold had brought the deer down and the white one with them but for myself I'm wondering. This year the tinkers hold their celebration of the coming of the Christ Child in the Finmory hills. My grandmother would have said the stag had come down to welcome them.'

'How could a stag know?' said Jinny quickly, pushing away Mr MacKenzie's words. She did not want a Christmas haunted by the tinkers' presence. She did not want to be involved in their powers of magic and mystery.

13

She wanted an ordinary Christmas holiday full of riding Shantih and presents and sitting round the fire with her family.

'If the tinkers are back Miss Tuke will be padlocking her ponies,' Jinny said glibly, and tightening her legs on Shantih's sides she sent her mare plunging forward, free from Mr MacKenzie's hold.

'It's rubbish,' Jinny told herself as she trotted after Mike. 'How could a wild stag be waiting for the tinkers?'

She glanced back over her shoulder and saw a wisp of smoke rising from Mr MacKenzie's bothy and she knew that the tinkers had arrived. Jinny shuddered suddenly, the touch of an icy hand on her spine. Was there a white stag? A white stag who waited for the tinkers' coming?

CHAPTER TWO

When Shantih and Bramble had finished their feeds, Jinny turned them out and ran through the winter debris of the overgrown Finmory garden to where the lighted kitchen shone golden in the greyness. At the front room window the Christmas tree that they had all decorated last night flickered with fairy lights. As she ran Jinny was thinking about lentil soup: possible, since she had asked Mike to request it, that it might be waiting for her – a mugful of lentil soup and a slice of her mother's homemade bread, and her prize.

'The first school prize I've ever won,' thought Jinny as she opened the kitchen door to find the kitchen overflowing with people. All her family were there. Petra was ironing and managing to look like a T.V. commercial, her mother was cutting a fruit cake, and sitting round the long kitchen table were her father with his balding head and ginger beard and Ken Dawson who was nineteen and lived with the family making pots with Mr Manders and growing fruit and vegetables for them all. Sitting opposite them was Miss Tuke, bursting from her unzipped anorak, her green wellies planted firmly on the stone floor and with her a youngish man with a thick black moustache whom Jinny didn't know.

'Full house,' said Mike grinning at her from the sink where he was filling two mugs with soup. 'I told them about your prize.'

Jinny checked quickly to see if they were laughing at her. They were not. Mike hadn't told them what a fool she had made of herself.

15

Listening with half an ear to their congratulations, for anything most people said about her talent for drawing was never the right thing, Jinny wondered why Miss Tuke had appeared so suddenly, so unexpectedly. Although Jinny looked on Bramble as her own pony, loved his dour hardiness second only to Shantih, she knew that he really belonged to Miss Tuke and that it was always possible that the phone might ring and it would be Miss Tuke demanding the return of her property. Over the rim of her mug Jinny stared at her suspiciously.

'Well,' asked Miss Tuke, 'let's have it. Out with your decision. Yes or no?'

'What?' said Jinny.

'Pardon,' corrected her mother and her father said that Jinny hadn't met Mr Redding and introduced her to the young man who leant across the table beaming.

'Delighted to meet you,' he said, grasping Jinny's distinctly dirty hand. 'You are going to be my third king, aren't you?'

'What?' said Jinny again.

'Don't tell me Dolina didn't ask you?' demanded Miss Tuke. 'Spent a small fortune on the phone to her last night. She is not the brightest.'

'She was trying to tell me. . .' began Jinny.

'I can see,' said Mr Redding, 'I had better explain. I'm your new minister,' and instantly Jinny recognized him. 'I've seen you around on that quite magnificent horse you ride.'

Jinny sat down paying proper attention, for anyone who appreciated Shantih was worth listening to.

'You might say it was your horse gave me the idea.'

'Warned you,' butted in Miss Tuke. 'You're asking for disaster.'

'Oh no. I really don't think so. Anyway Jinny, I've been working with Miss Broughton and her school children on a

16

nativity play. We're performing it in the church hall on Christmas Eve before the watchnight service. Unfortunately our three kings are all in quarantine for measles. What to do? Then I had this brilliant idea – the kings should ride up to the manger. Dolina comes to Bible Class and she has a pony. That's one. Then I phoned the trekking centre and here we are. Quite simply, will you be our third king?'

At first, when Mr Redding had spoken about a nativity play, Jinny had only thought of the usual children with tea towels tied round their heads and angels with drooping wings made from crepe paper and tinsel, but when Mr Redding mentioned Shantih Jinny's whole vision changed. She was the Golden King sitting astride a red-gold horse. Shantih would prance to the stable, mane and tail blown out into strands of light, her head carried high, honouring the Child. It would be the most terrific nativity play that Glenbost had ever seen.

'Oh I'd love to,' exclaimed Jinny. 'That would be ace!'

'Miss Tuke will ride, now who is it?'

'Easiest if I borrow Bramble. Save me carting one of my chaps all this way. And Dolina on their farm pony.'

'It should be two more Arabs,' thought Jinny. 'A grey and a black. The Grey King in silver and the Black King in purple. Not Dolina and Miss Tuke.' But she could ride Shantih in front of the others. She didn't need to look back at them.

'We're rather pushed for time,' said Mr Redding as Mrs Manders passed round cups of tea and put her cake on the table. 'Only three days till Christmas Eve. Could you both come along to church tomorrow? About twoish for a rehearsal?'

'No problem,' said Miss Tuke. 'I've no trekking bods staying with me this Christmas. Decided against it. Just as well seeing the tinks are back. Got to keep the beadies peeled when they're around.'

'And just what do you think they would do?' teased Mr Manders. 'Round up your ponies? Steal the silver cups?'

'Mock away,' said Miss Tuke. 'You'd have them all settled in detatched bungalows but I'd send the lot of them to prison first. I've seen them go through a farmyard with the farmer standing there and when he came to shut up his hens at night there would be three of them missing, boiling up in a tinker's pot, that's where they'd be.'

'Dad sees the tinkers as a social problem like the unemployed in Stopton and Tukey sees them as thieves in the night,' thought Jinny. 'They don't know them the way I do.' She swilled the last of her lentil soup round the bottom of her mug, thinking how strange it was that she should be the one to have known Keziah, who had been the wise woman of the tinkers before she died, and Tam the tinker boy who helped her to rescue Shantih and Bramble when they had been stolen.

'I think the tinkers are okay,' Jinny said but no one was listening to her.

'Not much fun travelling the roads in this weather,' said Mr Redding.

'Be a passerby,' said Ken killing the conversation because no one knew what he meant.

'Well,' said Mr Redding getting to his feet. 'I'll see you both tomorrow afternoon.'

'We really must try and come to church more often,' said Mrs Manders, and Mr Manders showed the minister out.

Before she went Miss Tuke warned Jinny not to feed Shantih too many oats; they didn't want her landing on top of the manger.

'Fancy you winning a prize,' said Petra when they had all gone.

18

'Fancy,' said Jinny and took her school bag upstairs to give it a decent burial until the day before school started again.

Jinny's room was the highest in Finmory House. From the hall, wide stairs led up to a long landing with bedrooms and bathrooms opening from it and at the end of the landing an almost vertical ladder of stairs went up to Jinny's own room.

An archway divided her room into two parts. One half of the room contained her bed, wardrobe and dressing table. Its windows looked down over the garden to the stables and the horses' field and on to the loop of sea, trapped between the jet black rocks of Finmory bay. The window in the other half of the room looked over the moors to the distant mountains. On the wall was a mural of the Red Horse plunging free from the confines of the wall, charging through blue and green branches heavy with white blossom. Its yellow eyes, burning from its head, were sparked to life by red pupils. On the other walls Jinny had pinned up the best of her own drawings and paintings.

Jinny swung her school bag under her bed and went to the window. Shantih and Bramble were standing at the field gate, rumps turned against the wind, waiting to be brought in.

'Don't care what Dad says,' Jinny decided. 'Don't care if they do eat more hay. I'm bringing them in.' Shantih had been blanket clipped in the autumn and although her coat had more or less grown in again, she still had to wear a New Zealand rug when she was out and be rugged up at night. Horsy relations of one of Jinny's school friends had lent her the rugs, and although Jinny was very grateful for them she would be glad when Shantih did not need them any longer.

Jinny went down to the stables that had been little more

than out-houses when they had first come to Finmory, but were now stalls, two loose boxes with a tack room and feed house. Teeth chattering with the cold, Jinny set square the two boxes, filled haynets and water buckets.

'Speed record,' she thought as she snatched up a halter and ran down to the field.

The horses were no longer at the gate.

'Shantih! Bramble!' Jinny shouted her surprise into the darkening afternoon and raced on to the field.

A skinny boy with a lurcher at his heels was crossing to the gate. Bramble, ears laid, tail switching, was bullying him for food while Shantih trotted high-stepping circles round them both.

'Tam!' cried Jinny.

Recognizing the tinker boy, she ran across the field to chase off the horses.

Half of Jinny was delighted to see him again, half furious that he should have come searching her out. Jinny thought it unlikely that he would just be dropping in for a cup of tea. She did not really want to be involved with the tinkers again. She wanted all her time free for the nativity play.

Tam's face was a paleness framed with black hair. His man's jacket and cut-down jeans hung loosely from his narrow frame.

'Chase them off,' Jinny told him. 'Don't let them bully you,' and she shouted at the horses, swinging the halter at Bramble and sending him off across the field in a sudden explosion of bucking hooves.

'I'm taking them in,' said Jinny and fitting the halter round Shantih's head she led her in to her box with Bramble trotting behind.

When both horses were in, Jinny turned to the silent Tam.

'Are you here for Christmas?' she asked him. 'Mr MacKenzie told us you were coming. How are you?'

Tam's black eyes stared at Jinny as her efforts at polite conversation washed over him.

'That's Zed, isn't it?' Jinny asked reaching down to Tam's dog but still Tam said nothing and Bramble kicked the side of his box demanding to be fed.

'Tell me what you're here for?' said Jinny in exasperation. 'It's too cold to stand here and I don't suppose you'll come into the house.'

'Sara sent me. She's waiting to see you.'

'Sara?'

'When Keziah went,' said Tam, naming the old tinker woman who had died last Easter, 'Sara took her place. She sent me to bring you. You are to ride your horse,' and Tam turned away walking with quick, light steps towards Mr MacKenzie's farm.

'I can't come just now,' said Jinny. 'They won't know where I've gone,' but despite her protests Tam didn't stop or look back. 'I can't come now,' she shouted after him.

But even as she spoke she was tipping Bramble's feed into his trough and grabbing Shantih's bridle.

Riding bareback, Jinny caught up with Tam as he climbed the hill to the bothy. Shantih was shying and spooking at the least thing, desperate to swing round and gallop back to where she had been forced to leave Bramble gutzying down his feed. As Jinny struggled to control her, Shantih's hooves caught in heather roots and stones that normally would have given way to her tread but were now frozen solid, snares for every step she took.

'Don't wait for me or anything like that,' Jinny snapped, thinking that she must be crazy to be battling over the moors just because some tinker woman she had never met wanted to see her.

As they reached the ruined bothy the door opened and a tall woman came out, silhouetted for a second by the firelight inside. The last time Jinny had been in the bothy

Keziah had been dying, and now a new wise woman was waiting for her.

Gathering Shantih in, Jinny paused, pushing her hair back from her face, swallowing hard. The things that made up her normal, everyday living – family and school, Miss Tuke and Bramble – lost their reality. As Jinny rode Shantih towards Sara the enchantment of the Red Horse which ruled the secret, mysterious part of her life, was the reality.

The tall woman had straight black hair as long as Jinny's own. She was younger than Keziah had been but her eyes held the same deep wisdom. As Shantih walked up to her Jinny felt the same singing delight, the same awe she had felt in Keziah's presence.

Sara laid her open hand on Shantih's shoulder and Jinny felt her horse relax, grow kind and gentle under Sara's touch.

'You come through the cold,' Sara said in a scraped rusty voice.

Jinny opened her mouth to echo some polite, empty agreement about the weather but couldn't speak. This was not the place for such quacking noise.

'Rider of a red horse, you must come when you are called. Be ready. From the white stag I sense despair. It is threatened by evil greed. Only the red horse you ride is swift enough to challenge it.'

The loud talk of three tinkers coming up the track to the bothy broke the spell. The bothy door was opened. 'Is that yourself, Charlie?' a woman's voice yelled out.

'Only the red horse you ride can save,' said Sara.

'What do you mean?' Jinny demanded, but Sara had turned away and Tam was nowhere to be seen.

The three tinkers were getting closer, supporting each other as they climbed the hill, laughing and shouting together. They were the tinkers that Miss Tuke knew

22

about. Jinny swung Shantih away, avoiding them, and rode home. She did not know what this Sara had meant with her talk of evil threatening the white stag.

By the time that Jinny had settled Shantih, her Finmory world was securely back in place. Thinking about tomorrow's rehearsal she had given Shantih an extra scoop of oats. Bringing Jinny's gift to the Child, Shantih must be light and air, a horse of fire scorning the earth.

It wasn't until she was going to bed that Jinny had time to think about Sara's words. Really think. Her evening had been filled with Petra boasting about all her party invitations and her mother making Jinny's favourite meal of cheese soufflé followed by chocolate peppermint ice cream, to celebrate Jinny's achievements.

'Sixth in your form and a special Art prize,' her father had said, toasting Jinny in a glass of raspberry wine. 'Very well done.'

'I've been top twice,' said Petra. 'You never make all this fuss about me.'

'But we do!' exclaimed her mother.

'I am the prodigal daughter,' said Jinny, 'and this is the fatted calf.'

'Great,' said Ken, who only ate grains, vegetables and fruit. No milk, no eggs, no cheese, nothing that was not given freely from the earth. 'Big deal for the calf.'

Jinny propped her elbows on the windowsill, leant her chin on her hands and stared out at the moonlit night. The moorland was petrified by the bitter cold, bleached by the full moon into a barren desert. Whatever Sara had meant when she had talked of despair, this landscape was the setting for it.

Suddenly Jinny was aware of movement on the hillside. Some five or six stags were crossing the moorland, their heads held stiffly upright as if in their branching antlers they held some priceless treasure that must be carried with great delicacy. Jinny watched, entranced – that they should be living wild and free. And then she saw another stag in front of them. Its coat shone milky pale and the spread of its branched antlers was greater than that of any of the other stags. It was the white stag.

High in the moon-clarity of the luminous night sky a helicopter racketed its way to the submarine base. Its noise made Jinny glance up at it and in that second the white stag had gone. Searching desperately Jinny could see no sign of it, only the other stags disappearing over a fold in the moors.

CHAPTER THREE

Jinny woke shivering with cold. Grey light told her it was early morning, before she dived under the bedclothes, tucking herself into a tight ball, rustling the sheets into a cosy parcelling about herself.

'Central heating,' thought Jinny wistfully. 'We should sell everything we don't absolutely need and get central heating. Sell Shantih? Oh yes, anything to be warm again,' and she grinned to herself, knowing that she would never sell Shantih.

The thought of the nativity play surfaced in her mind, how she would ride Shantih, dancing and golden. Then she remembered the white stag. For a moment Jinny could not be sure whether she had dreamt about the stag and then she remembered clearly – the other stags and the helicopter. It had not been a dream.

'Must see it again,' Jinny thought. 'Must go and look for it this morning.'

Miss Tuke was coming at half past one. If she was going to have time to ride Shantih over the moors she must get up now. Jinny burst out of bed, flinging the bedclothes from her and scrabbling into her clothes. In the kitchen she made coffee and gulped down the hot liquid as she pulled on her wellingtons, buttoned herself into her duffle and, tugging a woollen hat down over her ears, she dared her way outside.

Jinny stamped her feet on the icy ground, blotted out bare trees and sky with the clouds of her frozen breath. Shantih's whinny welcomed her into the warmth of the stable. She flung her arms over Shantih's withers and laid her cheek against the silken strength of the Arab's neck.

'Dear horse,' she said. 'No school. Finished. We're going to find the white stag. I saw it last night. At least I thought I did.'

Looking back Jinny couldn't be sure, couldn't be absolutely certain. Could it have been the moonlight shining on a perfectly ordinary stag?

Bramble clattered his hooves impatiently as Jinny mixed their feeds and tipped whispering oats, pony nuts and bran into their troughs, trying to remember just exactly what the stag had looked like.

When Ken and his grey dog Kelly came down to help her with the mucking out, she told him about the stag.

'Under the moon all things change,' he said. 'I used to think helicopters were friendly, bumbling things. Machines that had chosen to be a friend to man. I was rather fond of them until I saw one being used to fire at a target area. They'd managed to turn it into a killer too, same as all the rest. It's the metal vibes that do it.'

'Honestly!' Jinny exclaimed. 'I'm talking about a perfectly simple thing. Was the stag I saw last night white or did it just look white. Perfectly simple'.

'Nothing is simple,' said Ken. 'Or looked at in another way everything is.'

Hanging up Shantih's hay net, Jinny snorted with disgust. Always Ken had to go rooting or soaring for different meanings in the things you said; answering questions with other questions; stirring your mind until you were sure of nothing.

But Ken was the only one who understood about her drawings. How, when they were going right, it was not really Jinny who drew and painted them but something that flowed through her. Most people thought this was nonsense, for of course it was Jinny's hand that held the brush or pencil – but Ken understood. Jinny owed her life to Ken. If he had not found her when she had been lost in

26

a snow blizzard on the Finmory moors searching for Shantih, she would have lain down and slept in the snow. No Jinny, no Shantih.

'Don't be daft,' she said, then saw that Ken was laughing at her, his hazel eyes mocking her from his lean, tanned face.

'Well anyway,' stated Jinny,' I'm going to find it.'

It was after ten before Jinny had finished drying the dishes and, on her mother's insistence, making her bed and tidying her room.

'I'm nothing but a skivvy,' she thought, sitting forward over Shantih's withers, as her horse climbed a narrow sheep track carrying Jinny up onto the moors. 'Wonder if there was a housemaid once who lived in my room and knew the moors and the bay?'

Two hoodie crows creaked into flight making Shantih jump, skittering her hooves on the metalled ground.

'Steady,' warned Jinny. 'Come down on this and you'll break your legs.'

But Shantih refused to settle. The great pits of her nostrils dominated her fine-bred, porcelain-boned face. Her golden eyes drank in reflections of the moorland. Her ear tips touched in a maze of mane and forelock.

Jinny sat down hard in the saddle, her fingers playing with the reins so that Shantih's curbed energy sent her on, high stepping as a Lippizaner, each trotting stride held at the height of its arch.

They rose over a crest of moorland and saw in front of them a party of hinds. There were some twelve or fifteen deer with their rough coats burnished by the cold rays of the December sun. They were all grazing and for a moment Jinny was able to see them clearly, the detail of eye and rabbit mouth. Then with a sharp bark one of them gave the alarm. Heads jerked up, there was a split second of motionless panic and they were away, racing stick-legged out of sight.

Normally to have seen deer so close would have filled Jinny with utter delight but this morning she was searching for the white stag. Nothing less would do.

Knowing that the fleeing deer would have alerted any other creatures, Jinny let Shantih gallop, keeping her on the heather where the going, on the peaty soil, was less frozen. Once Shantih had got her wind out Jinny brought her back to a trot, then steadied her to a long, striding walk. She rode her over the moors, stopping at each high point to search for any sign of deer. Several times she saw hinds and once two stags, but they were all brown, shaggy, the colour of earth. They were not the white stag that Jinny had come to find.

As Jinny rode, the moorland fell away behind her. She could see beyond the bay, beyond the black pincher rocks to the reach and sway of the sea. Ahead were the pines and pewter water of Loch Varrich and in the distance the rock shards of the standing stones. The brief sun had been swallowed up by the heavy sky and a winter desolation stretched around her. All the farmers' sheep had been taken down to fanks close to the farms and Mr MacKenzie's Shetlands had made their own way down, hoping for hay.

Shantih, bored with walking, tossed her head restlessly, wanting to go home and Jinny remembered that Miss Tuke would be at Finmory at half past one. She would expect Bramble to be tacked up ready for her. Jinny looked at her watch, which suggested half past nine and meant she hadn't wound it up last night.

'Must be pretty late,' Jinny said aloud. 'Better get back,' and she turned Shantih, riding her down the steep hillside, suddenly aware of numb hands and aching feet.

She had not found the white stag. Stupid, in all this stretch of moorland, to have imagined for one minute that she would even catch a glimpse of it. If it existed. If it was no more than moonlight on red deer seen through the light of her imagination. Now they were going back the day was colder, more menacing. Jinny felt the mountains watching her. She urged Shantih on, unwilling to do more than walk when they were going downhill and the frozen ground was so treacherous.

'Not be long,' she lied to Shantih. 'Tukey will be in orbit if we're not there on time.'

Normally when Jinny spoke Shantih's ears flickered to the sound of her voice but now her ears were pointed sharply forward, her face adventuring on, as if she sought some purpose of her own and had forgotten Jinny's existence. Her walk changed to a jog, to a raking trot.

'Here!' warned Jinny, pulling on the reins. 'Watch it! Steady now!'

But Shantih totally ignored her. When Jinny tried to turn her towards Finmory, Shantih set her neck and went straight on, not fighting against Jinny but behaving as if she had no rider on her back. Only once before had Jinny known Shantih act like this – when she had carried Jinny to the place where the little stone age statue of a horse had been buried on the moor.

Remembering this Jinny let her reins fall loose on Shantih's neck, allowing herself to be taken where Shantih wanted to go.

They came to a hollow in the moor, surrounded on two sides by slides of fallen rock and scree, and on the third side by a rock face stepped with horizontal ledges. Sheltered from the wind it was warm as a summer's day. Dropping out of season Jinny dropped out of time. She felt Shantih stand with tail high and neck crested, whickering, in welcome or homage Jinny did not know which, as the white stag came round the side of the scree and stood in front of them.

Its white coat glowed luminous against the grey rock as

it stood, head high, proudly bearing its branching antlers. Holding her breath Jinny sat motionless. As if they were not separate, she experienced the wild freedom of the stag, totally alien to her own feeble living. Even when Shantih had been running wild on the moor or when she went bucking and rearing round her field, she did not have the fierce contained energy of the white stag.

A force, an urgency, linked stag and Arab horse and girl and in that moment Jinny sensed the stag's tension as if it sought to convey a great danger that was coming to the moor, the threat of evil that Sara had talked about. In her innermost self, more inner than senses or mind, Jinny felt the stag's distress and knew that Shantih was aware of it as well.

Almost instantly the stag turned and galloped away leaving Jinny thrown up on a beach after some deep, sea drowning. She stared after the stag, standing in her stirrups, straining to follow the glancing white shape that moved with a grace and speed almost beyond the range of human sight.

Jinny swung Shantih round forcing her upwards so that she could watch the white stag for as long as possible. From somewhere behind her there was the booming drone of an approaching helicopter.

'It's nothing,' Jinny told Shantih, speaking only with her mouth, the whole of her attention focused on the white stag. 'It's all right. You know what it is. Steady now.'

Shantih froze as the noise grew closer.

'Now don't start,' pleaded Jinny. 'Only a helicopter. You're used to them.'

But the noise was too close, too loud. Jinny looked over her shoulder and saw the helicopter coming straight towards her. It was far too low in the sky, so low that for a moment Jinny thought it was going to land beside her.

As it reached her Shantih sank down onto her quarters then reared, striking out with her forelegs. As she struggled to stay on top of Shantih and stop her breaking into a mad, break-neck gallop, Jinny lost sight of the white stag.

The helicopter passed over them and Shantih whirled in dervish panic, as Jinny dug her knees into the saddle and grasped a handful of mane in one hand. The helicopter roared on, flying low over the moor. A group of red deer, invisible before, sprang up from the heather and fled before it. As it quartered the moor, more deer burst from their shelter and joined the herd that, in a continual flow of head-high motion, raced in front of it.

'Devils!' Jinny shouted, sitting her rearing horse. 'Devils! Leave the deer alone! Stop it!' but although she yelled at the pitch of her lungs she could hardly hear her own voice for the noise of the machine.

It seemed as if the helicopter was going to drive the deer towards Ardtallon and then Jinny heard a blood chilling bellow – the white stag stood on an outcrop of rock, striking the stone with an imperious forefoot and swinging its head from side to side, challenging with a display of its magnificent antlers. It sprang down and, racing at the side of the herd of deer, it turned them away from the road that ran from Glenbost to Ardtallon, leading them back to the freedom of the hills.

The helicopter lifted and flew on until it was no more than a child's toy, then an almost invisible speck and was gone. The deer too had fled out of sight.

Jinny slid to the ground, hardly noticing the agony of her frozen feet, and leant trembling against Shantih, on the brink of tears.

'Devils from the submarine base. Devils to torment the deer like that. I'll tell the police,' she thought. 'I'll stop them somehow.'

And then she remembered a film she had seen where kangaroos were hunted from helicopters, the deadly zipp of rifle fire, the thud as the heavy bodies fell to the ground, and a blind terror flooded over Jinny in case the white stag should be harmed.

CHAPTER FOUR

'But I saw it,' insisted Jinny as she trotted Shantih towards Glenbost with Miss Tuke on Bramble bouncing beside her.

'Every village in the entire north of Scotland has one,' said Miss Tuke. 'People always know someone who has seen the white stag. Never seen it themselves.'

'But I saw it, I tell you.'

'They're usually hummels, regressive genes. Can't breed. No more white than white clay. No antlers either, or nothing worth speaking about. There isn't a tourist hasn't heard about white stags and that's about all they're good for, encouraging the tourists.'

'Mr MacKenzie told me about it.'

'And about the hill haggis?'

'Quite and utterly pointless talking about it,' Jinny told herself. 'The Tuke would only believe me if I brought the white stag home stuffed and then she'd say I'd painted it white.'

Her family hadn't been really interested either. Her father had been worrying about a broken element in his kiln. Mike had said that if the stag had been as close as all that, he hoped any fleas hadn't moved over for their Christmas holidays. Her mother had been too busy telling her that Miss Tuke would be here at any minute to pay attention to Jinny's news and Petra, as usual, had been practising her piano. Only Ken had listened, saying that stags had always been sacred animals, worshipped by man since earliest times.

'Only Ken,' thought Jinny, hardly hearing Miss Tuke's

opinion that deer were little better than rabbits and should be shot. 'Wonder if he'll go out and look for the stag himself?'

As they rounded a bend in the road a van the size of a furniture van was parked at the side of the verge. Shantih stopped dead, goggling in horror at such a monster that had never been there before and should certainly not be lurking there now.

'Get on with you,' muttered Jinny, sitting down hard, pushing Shantih on, forcing her to bound forward past the van.

Just as they were level with the cabin window the driver turned a page of the newspaper he was reading and shook out the paper to flatten it. Shantih sprang sideways, her hooves ringing on the frozen ground.

'Look out!' bawled Miss Tuke as Jinny's stirrup iron clashed against hers and Bramble burst forward shooting Miss Tuke out of the saddle.

Jinny caught a glimpse of the driver's tadpole face – webbed eyes, domed bald skull – startled from behind his paper as Shantih carried her past the van.

'Idiot girl!' raged Miss Tuke, shunting herself back into the saddle. 'How many times have I told you, you can't sit there dreaming when you're riding that spooker!'

'Oh,' said Jinny, shocked by the sudden attack. Then, supposing Miss Tuke was right, changed the subject quickly.

'Who was that driving the van?' she asked.

'Those geologists,' said Miss Tuke allowing herself to be sidetracked. 'I told you, they're staying in one of the summer cottages in Glenbost. No one really knows what they're doing. Very Government Secrecy Act and all that, but rumour has it that they're looking for somewhere to dump their filthy nuclear waste.'

'They shouldn't park their van so close to a corner,' said

Jinny and not wanting to listen to Miss Tuke telling her that it was Shantih's schooling and not the geologists' parking that was to blame, she touched her legs to Shantih's sides and sent her on into Glenbost.

The Church of Scotland, where Mr Redding was the minister, was a compact stone building, the kind of church a young child would draw, and beside it was the church hall where the nativity play was to be performed. A straight path led past Mrs Simpson's sell-all-things shop to the church gate where Dolina, sitting on Callum, was waiting for them.

Jinny stared in disgust at the shaggy, ungroomed Highland pony. As far as Jinny could make out Callum was a dark bay but she couldn't be sure, because his bristling winter coat was thickly clotted with dried mud, his small eyes looked out from a mud mask and his mane and tail grew rank in knots and entwinings of bracken. The leather of his bridle was dry and cracked and looked as if it had been pieced together from a carthorse's tackle.

'You might at least have brushed him!' exclaimed Jinny glaring at Dolina. Miss Tuke on Bramble was not Jinny's idea of a king but Dolina on Callum was just not possible.

'It is my mother is saying that this is the nonsense we're at. Thinking she is, of putting her foot down.'

'With both hands?' suggested Miss Tuke.

Dolina fixed Miss Tuke with the full blast of her mother's cod fish eyes.

'It is heathen, she says it is, bringing horses into a churchyard. And I would not be taking a brush to him when the mud is for keeping him warm outside. My father would not be wasting his money putting a pony in a stable,' and Dolina made the noise, half snort, half scoffing laugh, that she always made when she felt she had pointed out the obvious to a total imbecile.

'Well you'll need to groom him for the real play,' stated Jinny.

'Ah, grand to see you,' called Mr Redding, coming down the path in sheepskin jacket and check trousers, looking more like an amiable social worker than a minister. 'How about putting your horses into the field and coming into the hall. You're not on until the grand finale. Be rather arctic waiting out here?'

'How's your beast for kicking?' Miss Tuke demanded, looking suspiciously at Callum.

'Callum would not be at the kicking if it were the volcano exploding behind him,' stated Dolina smugly.

'Then that's the plan,' and Miss Tuke turned Bramble and rode towards the field which Jinny and Mike used during term time.

When they had turned their horses loose they stood for a moment in case there should be a kicking match but Dolina was right. Even when Bramble went storming up to Callum, in a high, floating trot, snorting his suspicions of a strange pony, Callum just kept on grazing.

'Did I not say?' said Dolina and they all went into the church hall, stamping frozen feet and clutching their hands under their arms.

'Come now,' called Mr Redding to the twenty or so children who were racing round the hall. 'Now we're all here let's get settled. That's the way. Good. Very good. Sit down. All settle.'

Miss Broughton, the Glenbost Primary School teacher, joined Mr Redding, clapping her hands smartly. The noise stopped so suddenly that everyone was able to hear Dolina informing Miss Tuke that her mother had never known such goings on.

'We do have a nativity play every Christmas,' Miss Broughton told Dolina. 'Not in the least unusual.'

'Not with the horses,' muttered Dolina, staring down at her hands.

'Ready choir?' said Miss Broughton and she organized her choir of angels into a row across the front of the hall, leaving space behind them for the cardboard box that was the manger. Behind the manger were the high double doors that would be opened for the arrival of the kings.

Mr Redding, coming to sit next to Miss Tuke, handed out carol sheets.

'We want everyone to join in,' he said, and his booming voice joined Miss Tuke's foghorn praise as they sang the first verse of "O little town of Bethlehem", completely drowning the angels.

Then Mary and Joseph walked slowly up the centre of the hall singing a duet of question and answer as they approached Bethlehem. Mary's voice was high and clear, Joseph's an embarrassed mumble.

'Joseph, louder!' encouraged Miss Broughton.

'Shout it out, boy,' echoed Miss Tuke. 'Can't hear you.'

They reached the row of angels and an innkeeper appeared from behind them.

'Good woman, I implore you

Afford my wife a bed,' mumbled Joseph.

'Nay, nay I've nothing for you

Except the cattle shed,' said the innkeeper.

'Can't sing a note,' confided Mr Redding, 'but terribly keen, we had to give her a part,' and Jinny knew how it was.

Mary and Joseph followed the Innkeeper behind the row of angels and nothing else happened. The choir looked round doubtfully. Someone seized by the giggles exploded.

'Really!' Miss Broughton snapped. 'Come along now. Only two days until we're performing in front of an audience. Angels, this is where the lights go out and you sing by yourselves. "How silently, how silently the wondrous gift is given." Ready?'

37

'We can't,' said one of the angels. 'They haven't got Jesus.'

'Why not? Didn't you bring him, Sandra?' demanded Miss Broughton.

'He's smashed. My wee sister dropped him on the kitchen floor and his head's all smashed.'

'Well don't cry about it,' brisked Miss Broughton as tears began to trickle down Sandra's plump cheeks. 'Does anyone else have a baby doll we could borrow?'

Several mothers had gathered to watch from the back of the hall and one of them promised a suitable doll.

'Lovely,' said Miss Broughton and Mr Redding folded a blanket round a cushion and placed it in the box that was being the manger until the dress rehearsal, when the tea chests containing the nativity things would be brought up from the church cellar.

Jinny was thinking about the white stag. How had Shantih known where it would be? What was it that was troubling the stag? She was only conscious of the nativity play as if it were on television when she wasn't really watching it.

Miss Broughton reorganized her choir into singing "Silent Night" and when they had finished they stood back to let Mary and Joseph and the manger come into view.

Sweet and true, Mary sang "Joseph dearest, Joseph mine, Help me rock this Child divine". The angels stepped into line again and while everyone sang "While shepherds watched their flocks by night", several self-conscious shepherds carrying toy lambs and crooks came down the centre of the hall to settle on the floor in front of the angels.

In her mind Jinny recreated the image of the white stag, joining details of nostril and eye, straight neck, slab sides with their rough matting of coarse white hair, metal strong legs and razor-sharp, cloven hooves. She saw the stag clearly, its antlers branching majestically upward above the calm brow.

'I had hoped we might have had a real sheep,' Mr Redding said. 'But Mrs McKay who looks after our church so well, was not too keen.'

A tall, fair-headed boy whom Jinny didn't know, came forward and stood in front of the angels, announcing Christ's birth to the shepherds.

'Fear not: for, behold, I bring you good tidings of great joy, which shall be to all people.
For unto you is born this day in the city of David a Saviour, which is Christ the Lord.'

As his words sang out Jinny was filled and lifted by them.

'And this shall be a sign unto you; ye shall find the babe wrapped in swaddling clothes and lying in a manger.'

The shepherds whispered conversations amongst themselves, which Miss Broughton made them repeat three times without managing to make them speak any louder, and then gathering up their belongings they set off up the hall to find the manger.

As Jinny watched entranced, the irridescent image of the white stag faded and she seemed to be sitting high up in a gallery looking down onto a stage where the choir angels blazed in glory, all colours and no colours. Mary and Joseph were enamelled figures from an icon, and the manger a burning light. The shepherds waited on a hillside that was the bitter Finmory moors, nowhere, yet everywhere, having no place. Above them all hung the fiery hawk-angel, wings outspread proclaiming the gift of great joy that was to be for all men, for all time.

The shepherds returned, the angels divided to make a

passageway to the manger and the shepherds knelt, hastily depositing their gifts of lambs and crooks, and everyone sang "The First Nowell".

'Now, how about a break for a cuppa,' said Mr Redding clapping his hands for attention. 'Lemonade for you all, then back to your places for the arrival of the Kings. You are all doing wonderfully well.'

'I'm glad you think so,' laughed Miss Broughton. 'They will not speak out and I've told them until I'm sick of telling them.'

Shocked back to the present Jinny stared about her at the dingy church hall, the ordinary children, the rug abandoned in its box. She looked quickly at the three adults and Dolina.

'Didn't you see it?' she demanded of Mr Redding, for he was a minister who must know about these things. 'See the light and the angels?'

Mr Redding looked across at Jinny, vaguely, kindly. 'Angels?'

'I thought I could see them. Well not really see them, sort of imagining how it really was in Bethlehem.'

Jinny stared at their lightless faces and knew they had no idea what she was talking about. But it didn't matter. Only one thing mattered – to make the Glenbost nativity play the very best the village had ever seen. The three kings must be magnificent. She must be the Golden King and Shantih her horse of fire.

'Lemonade or tea, Jinny?' asked Miss Tuke and Jinny chose lemonade.

'We'll be off to tack up,' said Miss Tuke gulping down hot tea. 'Now, what exactly do you want us to do?'

'I'm having two spotlights fixed up,' explained Mr Redding. 'I want the three of you to wait at the foot of the path that leads to the double doors. When we start to sing "We Three Kings of Orient Are", two of the children will open the doors and you will all ride up to the hall.'

'Will they be able to see us inside?' asked Miss Tuke.

'Yes, I've checked. Luckily the path slopes down to the doors, so no problem.'

'Good-o,' said Miss Tuke.

'I understand we have costumes for a Golden King.'

'Shantih,' demanded Jinny just in case Miss Tuke should have any notions of grandeur. 'Shantih must be the Golden Horse.'

'Of course,' agreed Mr Redding. 'And Miss Tuke carrying frankincense, wearing a silver costume?'

'If I can persuade my portly person to fit into it.'

'Dolina, the Black King bringing the dark gift of myrrh?'

'My mother . . .' began Dolina but Mr Redding was not listening.

'You'll all ride up to the hall while we sing the first verse,' began Mr Redding.

'Jinny's raver will probably charge straight into the hall,' interrupted Miss Tuke, twinkling at Jinny over her tea cup.

'Then during the chorus,' continued Mr Redding, pointing to the carol on his sheet, 'Jinny will dismount, offer her gift at the manger while everyone sings the verse "Born a King on Bethlehem's plain, Gold I bring to crown him again", then back to her horse.'

'Right,' said Jinny seeing in her mind's eye how she would kneel with her gold cloak falling about her and Shantih standing behind her.

'Miss Tuke, you'll dismount during the next chorus and take your gift of frankincense to the manger while we sing "Frankincense to offer have I . . ." When you're back with your horse, Dolina will dismount during the next chorus and she offers her gift while we sing "Myrrh is mine . . ." Then a last chorus.'

'Who will hold the horses?' asked Miss Tuke.

'Mrs Bowen has very kindly promised us her daughter Amanda to be our horse holder. She's staying with friends until tomorrow but she will be here on the night and she might make the dress rehearsal.'

'Bowen,' thought Jinny, then she remembered the lady on the bay horse who had won the showing class at Inverburgh Show last Easter. Any daughter of hers would be quite capable of holding Shantih.

'Then we all sing,

> "What can I give Him Poor as I am.
> If I were a shepherd I would bring a lamb.
> If I were a wise man I would do my part.
> Yet what I can I give him—Give my heart."'

sang Mr Redding. 'And that's when any children in the audience can bring their gifts. I've asked for simple toys which we can send off to Ethiopia. Finally, "O Come All Ye Faithful" belted out by everyone. I'll ask a blessing and then we all go into church for the watchnight service.'

Mr Redding smiled, smooth and confident, beaming forth reassurance. As long as he was there everything would be all right.

'My mother says,' began Dolina but Miss Tuke was zipping up.

'Ready kings?' she asked. 'Trek forward,' and with Jinny and Dolina scurrying to catch up she marched out of the hall.

Shantih came galloping to the field gate, greeting Jinny with a thunderous whinny.

'She thinks she's going home,' Jinny realized, foreseeing trouble. But it was Callum who jibbed at the church gate, refusing to move. Even when Miss Tuke grabbed his bridle and rode Bramble forward, Callum

42

stayed rooted to the spot, only his neck concertinaed on.

'Och it is the farm beast he is,' said Dolina sourly. 'He is not used to such carryings on. If it were the ploughing we were at he would be making the mincemeat out of the two of you.'

She slumped off Callum's back, threw herself at his shoulder knocking him off balance and forcing him to step forward.

'Get on you varmint,' she yelled and she hammered him with clenched fists on his mud caked shoulder.

'Advancing under a smoke screen?' asked Mr Redding but Dolina only scowled at him. 'Right I'll let them know you're here,' and the minister walked up to the doors and banged loudly on them.

Quite clearly they heard the words of the carol and the doors of the hall were pushed open.

'Walk,' commanded Miss Tuke looking at Jinny. 'No going off like the hammers,'

They rode together to the hall, Jinny controlling Shantih's desire to gallop, holding her to a spring-hoofed walk. While Jinny offered her imaginary gift Shantih stood goggling suspiciously into the hall, Miss Tuke's hand on the rein controlling her. But when "O Come All Ye Faithful" was roared out Shantih sprang back, almost pulling her reins from Jinny's grip.

'Idiot,' Jinny told her, ignoring Miss Tuke's hard look. 'It's only a carol. My favourite one.'

'Everyone together,' encouraged Mr Redding and knowing her tuneless voice wouldn't be heard next to Miss Tuke, Jinny joined in.

'O come let us adore Him,
 O come let us adore Him,
 O come let us adore Him, Christ the Lord.'

Their singing flowed from the brightly lit hall out over the silent moors. The winter sky, barred with jade and amethyst cloud, was lit by the afterglow of the setting sun. Bare trees around the church were etched against its light. And Shantih was the horse of the Golden King. Once they all had their costumes the play would come to life.

'It must be the very best possible play,' Jinny promised herself.

'One thing certain,' said Miss Broughton. 'We'll need to have another rehearsal tomorrow. Next afternoon is the dress rehearsal and then it's Christmas Eve.'

Miss Tuke, announcing that her ponies would be kicking jolly lumps out of each other if she didn't get back to give them their hay, agreed to come.

'Bit of a dog's dinner,' she said to Jinny as they trotted full out for Finmory.

'But it will be good,' Jinny insisted, 'because Shantih is in it.'

When they passed Mr MacKenzie's yard several tinkers were standing talking to him.

'Can't think why he encourages them,' snorted Miss Tuke. 'I'd chase out the lot of them.'

One of the tinkers was Sara. She turned at the sound of the horses and looked straight at Jinny, paying no attention to Jinny's feeble 'Hello.'

Although the tinker woman did not speak Jinny heard her voice ringing clearly in her mind.

'The white stag is threatened by evil greed . . . Be ready.'

But when Jinny looked back Sara had turned away and was walking up the hill towards the bothy. Shuddering, Jinny remembered the distress she had sensed from the stag; a fear of things to come.

CHAPTER FIVE

Before breakfast next morning, Jinny had mucked out Shantih and Bramble, fed them, turned Bramble out and left Shantih pulling at her hay net. Jinny raced back into the house her head full of plans to find the white stag again only to discover to her dismay that all her family were sitting down to breakfast.

'Bother it,' she thought. 'Now I'll need to do the dishes or go for the milk or something.' She had been hoping to make herself a quick coffee and a slice of toast and get back to Shantih before anyone saw her.

'You're on the move this morning,' smiled her mother. 'Would you like a boiled egg?'

'Okay. Thanks,' said Jinny helping herself to muesli and thinking her mother was being extra bright.

Mrs Manders set the boiled egg in front of Jinny and Petra said 'Well you'd better tell her.'

'What?' demanded Jinny. 'Go on tell me the worst.'

'It's not the worst,' said Petra. 'Stop trying to dramatize everything. It's only that you've to go into Glenbost with Dad to do the shopping while he goes on to Ardtallon to see the plumber. Which means that you won't have time to go gadding about on the hills.'

'It is your turn,' said Mike. 'And I can't go because Mr MacKenzie is having the vet to his cows this morning and I've got to be there.'

'And I'm going to the hairdresser in Inverburgh to have my hair done for tomorrow night,' said Petra.

'Be a mess before you get to your bloomin' party,' scowled Jinny. 'Oh I can't go. I'm going to look for the white stag again. I can't possibly go.'

45

But despite all her protests, later in the morning, Jinny found herself getting out of the car at Mrs Simpson's shop with shopping bags and a long shopping list.

'Please do be as quick as you can,' Jinny said despairingly to her father but she had no hope. Mr Blair, the plumber, was a man who never used one word when a hundred would do, and on the subject of Finmory drains there was plenty to be said.

Jinny walked toe to heel up to Mrs Simpson's shop. She had nearly reached the door when it was flung open and three men came out. They were talking together and didn't see Jinny until they had almost bumped into her.

'Don't mind me,' Jinny muttered, wondering who they were.

One of the men turned to look at her and she recognized the bald, tadpole shaped head with its sucker lips and half closed eyes. It was the man who had been in the van yesterday. They must be the geologists. She looked curiously at them but they hurried on without speaking.

Jinny shrugged her shoulders and marched into Mrs Simpson's. To her dismay the shop was busy. Four Glenbost housewives were standing drinking in Mrs Simpson's words.

'Bloomin' not my day,' thought Jinny. Any hopes she had left of searching out the white stag were fading rapidly.

'Yes, it is the wee bit trade I have had from them. I will not be denying it,' said Mrs Simpson settling her floral bosom on the counter. 'But not one name do I have for them, and not one letter has been coming for them. Is that not strange when they are from the government?'

Mrs Simpson's audience clucked their agreement.

'It is very particular they are in the things they buy.

46

The Smiler now, I would say myself it is the butchering he has been at. Asking for the foreign English cuts of meat and coming behind me to the cold store to be showing me how he wanted it chopping.'

Jinny stopped listening. Mrs Simpson's cold store was a small room at the back of her shop with a freezer in it. Before she had known any better Jinny had once gone to fetch mince from the freezer for Mrs Simpson. When she had opened the freezer door, a half sheep with its head still on had gazed mournfully out at her. Jinny shivered at the memory. She hated the thought of animals being killed for food.

Instantly she switched her mind away from the unthinkable facts of slaughterhouses and transportation ships. To think, really think, about such things would bring her safe, secure, card-pack world fluttering down about her. Perhaps Petra was right. Perhaps it was better not to think about things like that in case they upset you. Better not to look.

Seeing a pile of new books Jinny searched through them. Quite often Mrs Simpson would buy horsy ones with Jinny in mind.

"Thunderhead," by Mary O'Hara was the last book in the pile. "My Friend Flicka" was one of Jinny's favourite books and she had been searching for ages for "Thunderhead", its sequel. But this copy was a hardback. Jinny opened it urgently, saw the horrendous price of £5.50 and knew that she couldn't possibly afford it. Christmas presents had used up nearly all her money. She would need to persuade her father to buy it for her.

Lugging her full shopping bags Jinny set off towards Ardtallon. If she waited for her father outside the shop there wouldn't be enough time to tell him how vital it was for her to have "Thunderhead" at once, but if she walked towards Ardtallon, he would pick her up before the shop and she could explain to him how desperately she wanted the book.

Half an hour later Jinny was still waiting. She had reached the last of the village crofts. If she went any further there would be nowhere to shelter should the louring clouds turn to snow. Furiously Jinny stamped her frozen toes and thought how she might have been riding Shantih.

'Come on. Hurry up,' she muttered and saw to her dismay a hailstorm advancing across the moor in a blinding fall of white. Jinny dashed for shelter into the doorway of the whitewashed croft. As she waited tucked into the angle of the porch, she heard voices from inside the croft. Jinny had thought the croft was empty, since it was one of the holiday cottages that were only used in the summer.

For a second she didn't know what to do. If whoever was inside came out and found her, what would she say? But no one could possibly expect her to stand in the middle of the road being hailed on when she could shelter by the croft.

Jinny could hear the drumming noise of the hailstorm as it marched towards her over the moor. She thought of dashing back to shelter in another doorway but knew there wouldn't be time.

From inside the croft a man's voice was saying something about Christmas Eve. Jinny stared down the road wishing her father would appear.

'One o'clock for the drop,' the man said. 'Loaded up by two and over the border . . .' Then Jinny saw their car. Grabbing up her shopping bags she ran into the road shouting. Her father stood on his brakes and the car skidded to a halt.

'What the dickens are you doing here?' he demanded, throwing open the passenger door. 'Might easily have missed you. Or hit you!'

Jinny bundled into the car hauling her shopping in behind her, as the hailstorm burst upon them.

'A white out,' said Jinny as the hail blotted out all the car windows, shutting them into a grey half light.

As suddenly as it had come the hail passed over, leaving the moors towards Ardtallon frosted under a clear sky.

Jinny explained about the book.

'Not even if it was 50p,' said her father driving steadily past Mrs Simpson's. 'If Mr Blair's opinion of our plumbing is correct we will have to sell all the books we possess rather than buy new ones.'

'I put it at the bottom of the pile,' said Jinny remembering that it was nearly Christmas. 'Just in case Father Christmas should be looking for it.'

But Father Christmas didn't appear to have heard.

'In no time at all it'll be Christmas,' Jinny thought. 'Not tomorrow night but the next, Shantih will be the Golden Horse.'

Miss Tuke was very late. Jinny waited for her impatiently, holding Shantih and Bramble in readiness for instant departure, but it was ages before Miss Tuke's trekking van rattled into the drive.

'One of the little blighters got himself kicked. Had to stop and see to it,' she explained as she settled her hard hat on her head and climbed aboard Bramble.

When they reached the church hall "While Shepherds Watched" was carolling out to greet them.

'Humph,' said Miss Tuke. 'Hardly worth taking their tack off. Nip in and see what Mr Redding thinks.'

Jinny handed her reins to Miss Tuke and went into the hall. Dolina was standing just inside the door.

'It was Miss Tuke's fault,' said Jinny expecting Dolina to be mad with her for being so late.

'My mother,' said Dolina, 'has put her foot down. I am to have no more to do with it.'

Jinny stared at her in dismay.

'You mean you're not going to be a king? You're not going to ride Callum?'

'I am to have no part in such nonsense.'

'But you can't! You can't! There's got to be three kings!'

'I was only hanging on to tell you. Mr Redding is not bothered.'

'But I am,' cried Jinny. Dolina and Callum wouldn't have been much but without them the nativity play would be a nonsense. 'You've got to. You said you would and you've got to.'

Shepherds and angels were all listening to Jinny. Mr Redding and Miss Broughton came across the hall towards them.

'Well I am not,' said Dolina and stomped out.

'We'll find someone else. Perhaps I could be the third king on foot,' consoled Miss Broughton.

'That would be no use,' said Jinny desperately. 'There's got to be a horse for a king.'

'Let's discuss it when we have tea,' suggested Mr Redding. 'Some of the children have to go home early today so we just went straight ahead. You're nearly on. Would you like to go round and be ready to ride up the path?'

'This is stupid,' thought Jinny, on the edge of sulking. 'Me and the Tuke, what use is that?'

'Rope in Petra or Mike?' suggested Miss Tuke when she heard that Dolina had abandoned them.

'Petra's going to a party and Mike isn't interested,' stated Jinny.

This time Shantih stood calmly while Jinny presented her gift. As she came back to take Shantih's reins and stand with her Jinny was caught again in the tissue of her dream, the aching longing that theirs should be a celebration worthy of the Christ Child, that the Child in

50

his winter stable should be welcomed into the world by the best nativity play possible.

'But two Kings!' thought Jinny in disgust and then she thought, 'Ken?' but she knew there wasn't much chance. Ken thought most churches were like prisons and hospitals, places that destroyed the spirit. But perhaps she would ask him. You could never be sure of Ken. Ken as the Black King would be right.

CHAPTER SIX

Next morning Jinny left nothing to chance. She was up before any of her family and took a mug of coffee and two slices of toast down to the stable with her.

'Great, greedy horse,' she told Bramble as the Highland almost knocked her over, barging in to get his feed as Jinny was tipping it into his trough. 'There you are. There's no one else going to touch it.'

Bramble wizened his nostrils and dived into his feed but Shantih waited courteously, stepping aside to let Jinny into her box and standing patiently while Jinny emptied the feed into her trough. She breathed over the dry oats, picking fastidiously at pony nuts, searching for strips of carrot.

'I've got my breakfast here,' Jinny told her. 'And then we're going out on the moors. Will you find the white stag for me? Take me to it again?'

For a second Shantih stopped chewing, regarded Jinny with a wise eye.

'What do you know?' whispered Jinny, smoothing Shantih's mane, running her hand down her sleek neck. 'How did you know the stag would be there?'

But there was no way Shantih could tell her. Jinny picked up the empty bucket and went out to eat her breakfast.

'Stable service?' asked Ken, appearing unexpectedly round the stable door.

'Could be,' said Jinny and gave him a piece of her toast.

She hadn't had a chance to speak to him last night. Over supper hadn't seemed a good time and then Ken had gone to his room which meant that he was not to be disturbed. She would need to ask him now, for she had to let Miss Tuke know what was happening.

'You're up early,' she said to Ken.

'Comes from spending the night reading "Lord of the Rings". See myself as Tom Bombadil. "Old Tom Bombadil is a merry fellow, bright blue his jacket is and his boots are yellow",' quoted Ken tapping his feet and twirling neatly round. '"Tom Bombadil is the Master".'

'Good mood,' thought Jinny but before she had time to ask, Ken said, 'I'll be your third King.'

'How did you know?'

'Magic,' mocked Ken. 'Your mum asked me.'

'That would be absolutely super if you would. Miss Tuke says she'll bring one of her trekking ponies over and you can be the Black King on Bramble. I never thought you would, you know. You're not usually keen on things like this, are you?'

Ken's green brown eyes laughed at Jinny. 'You mean I'm not much of a Christian?'

'Well . . . You're not, are you?'

'No one in your family goes to church much and I should reckon I read the Bible more than they do. It's the same as all the other books of power, shouting out the way it is. Only no one listens. They go to church instead. Anyway adoring the Child is different. Pagan, worshipping the light. Taking gifts.'

'Myrrh for you,' said Jinny bringing Ken back to earth before he got started.

'Myrrh! Phew! Not today. No place for your myrrh, whatever it was. Need more than myrrh to welcome the New. Got to find something worth offering, something that costs.'

'That's what the headmaster told us,' said Jinny remembering her headmaster's challenge – that they should find something they were afraid of and take a long, hard look at it.

'Anyway,' said Jinny getting up from the bale of straw she had been sitting on. 'That's smashing if you'll be a king. Will you phone Miss Tuke?'

'Are you moving on?'

'I'm going to look for the white stag again.'

'More! More!' groaned Ken.

'Am,' said Jinny and went off to start mucking out.

'I'll go towards Ardtallon,' she thought half an hour later, when she was climbing over the moor, away from Finmory. 'Don't know that way so well.'

Shantih was fresh, plunging and dancing as she made her way across the moor, leaping over the low stone walls at a touch from Jinny's legs, soaring into the air from a walk, desperate to gallop on.

'You'll charge right into the hall,' thought Jinny, knowing it was the extra oats she had been giving Shantih, and she imagined herself jumping over the manger, charging through the angels and scattering the audience.

As she rode, her eyes were skinned for the least movement of deer.

'Be lovely if they came down so close to the house all the year round,' she thought. 'I would see the fawns. Tame them.'

Jinny switched back her hair, furious with herself. It would be the worst possible thing for the deer if they were to become tame. The best for them was that they should stay wild and free. Best for people too, that the deer should be independent, half glimpsed on the skyline, a sudden touch of beauty that lit up an ordinary day with the reminder of the otherness of things.

Jinny rode on for about a hour, seeing parties of hinds in the distance and once the branched silhouette of a stag. There was no sign of the white stag nor did Shantih show any awareness of its presence. She walked spring-heeled, looking about her but accepting Jinny's aids without any will of her own.

Jinny heard the helicopter behind her, glanced back over her shoulder, shuddering goose-over-her-grave as she remembered how it had swooped over her before.

'Hope it's not the same lunatics,' she muttered to Shantih, her fingers imperceptibly gathering in the reins, her seat pressing tighter into the saddle as she waited, her spine tingling to the approaching noise.

'It is!' thought Jinny desperately. 'It's the same one,' and in a second the mechanical fury was upon her.

Shantih laid her ears, set her neck and with a half rear was away galloping low and possessed, her mind taken from her, unable to do anything but flee from this destruction.

Jinny yanked viciously at the bit, tugging with both hands on one rein as she fought to turn Shantih from the path of the helicopter. As she struggled Jinny was aware of the deer fleeing in front of her. Like fire over tinder-dry grass they flickered and leapt, as the terror of the helicopter drove them on.

'Stop!' Jinny screamed. 'Oh Shantih, stop! Shantih stop it! Whoa horse! Whoa!' but her screaming hysteria had no effect on Shantih's breakneck speed.

Racing over the frozen ground Shantih stumbled, regained her footing and charged on. She cleared a low wall, then stretched out to clear the spread of fallen stones on the other side.

Jinny crouched helplessly. There was nothing she could do except hang on. She had no strength to fight against Shantih's blind panic.

'Why doesn't it pass us?' she thought. 'Why is it staying behind us?'

It was as if the helicopter was a mechanical sheepdog,

driving them purposefully before it, roaring from side to side, steadily increasing the number of deer that fled before it towards Ardtallon.

Suddenly Shantih fell. One second at full gallop, the next, catching a front hoof in a snare of heather she came crashing down. Her face hit the ground, her quarters and hind legs rose in the air behind her, as spectacular as a steeplechaser's fall. Thrown clear into a brittle, pin cushion of heather, Jinny lay face downwards sobbing with fury. Who were they, these mad men, who took pleasure out of tormenting the deer? How dare they fly over the moors like that, terrifying them for their twisted sense of pleasure.

Jinny pushed herself to her feet again and dashed to where Shantih stood with her head hanging and her sides clapped in. Holding her breath for fear of what she might find, Jinny ran her hands down Shantih's legs and under her belly, felt urgently over her head and back but there was no blood. Grasping the bit ring Jinny urged Shantih forward, moved her about but her horse was sound.

'Dear God,' she said throwing her arm over Shantih's withers, butting her head against Shantih's neck. The fear that Shantih might have been harmed filled her eyes with tears. 'Oh thank you, God.' For so easily going at that speed over the frozen ground she could have injured herself, broken her leg, her back. But only her nose was scratched where it had hit the ground.

Jinny slipped her arm through Shantih's reins and saw the helicopter rise from the herd of deer it had gathered and clatter off in the direction of the submarine base.

'Bloomin' wonder how often he does this,' Jinny thought furiously. She was sure it wasn't allowed, was not legal to harass deer like that. Surely other people must have seen it and reported it to the police. But the villagers and farmers were used to seeing helicopters crossing to the base. Maybe they were only doing it just now, taking advantage of the empty moors when all the sheep had been taken down close to the farms and there was no one on the hills to see them. They wouldn't dare do it when the sheep were on the moors.

'Sport,' thought Jinny, beside herself with rage. 'That's what they'd call it – sport!'

Shantih was streaked with sweat, her mane and tail wisped and her chest and belly curded white.

'Poor horse,' said Jinny looking at her wretched state not knowing whether she should lead her part of the way back or whether she could ride her. One thing was certain she would take some grooming to turn her into a king's horse for that afternoon. 'Oh Shantih! Oh horse!'

Deciding that her weight didn't really make any difference to Shantih and that there would be less chance of her catching cold if she rode her, Jinny mounted and stared about her trying to get her bearings.

She was almost at Ardtallon, so there would be no way down to the road, for here the moors dropped in a sheer fall of rock to the ground at the side of the road.

'Engage jump power,' thought Jinny and tucked her knees under Shantih's great, feathered wings.

Last summer she had ridden round the road to Ardtallon to see Dolina. They had gone for a picnic on the moors. Dolina had insisted that the almost vertical track up the side of the rock was only a dawdle but Jinny had been terrified as she had led Shantih up it. She had gone home over the moors swearing nothing would ever make her take Shantih down the track to the road.

'Och Callum would be skipping along it,' Dolina had insisted, but when Jinny had tried to find out how often Callum had actually skipped his way down, Dolina had become rather vague.

'Bet he never came down it,' Jinny thought. 'Maybe up

it but never down,' and she certainly wasn't going to risk taking Shantih down it now.

She was just about to turn and retrace the steps of their crazed stampede when she saw three men standing together, close to where the helicopter had lifted from the deer.

Although Jinny couldn't make out who they were she was sure they must be farmers, for who else would be on the moors in this cold? And even if they weren't farmers they must have seen the helicopter buzzing the deer and would be witnesses to prove that Jinny's story wasn't an exaggeration.

Jinny walked Shantih towards them waving to them, the first time naturally but after that awkwardly, not sure whether they had seen her or not.

As Jinny reached them one of the men stepped forward.

'Did you see the helicopter?' Jinny demanded. 'Did you see what it was doing? Chasing the deer!'

'They're easily scared,' said the man, ignoring Jinny's distress.

'Of course they're scared when the helicopter is down so low . . .' began Jinny indignantly.

'Do you know you're trespassing?' asked the man, his slit mouth setting free his words as if they were miser's silver.

'Trespassing!' exclaimed Jinny in astonishment. She had always ridden Shantih all over the moors around Finmory and this was the first time that anyone had mentioned trespassing.

'Of course I'm not!' Jinny replied indignantly. 'I can ride where I like. All the farmers know me.'

'From now on this part of the moor is being taken over for government purposes,' said another of the men coming forward. 'So keep away from it.'

In the cold the man's sucker lips had a blueish tinge and

58

his half closed eyes swam in pools of moisture and at once Jinny recognized them as the geologists.

'Whenever we get the rest of the wire and the posts we'll be fencing it off,' said the slit mouthed man gesturing to a roll of barbed wire that was lying on the ground.

Jinny stared at it, not believing him. She was sure that if there was any possibility of the moors being taken over by the government the village grapevine would have heard about it.

'So off you go,' said the tadpole man. 'And don't come near here again.'

'I'm going,' said Jinny, 'because I'll be late for the dress rehearsal if I don't. Not because you're telling me to go and I'll ask the police whether I can ride here.'

'Cheek of them, telling me where I can ride,' Jinny muttered as she rode away towards Finmory. 'Bloomin' cheek.'

She shivered, nervously aware of how isolated she was. Surrounded by the bleak distances of moorland anything could have happened to her and no one would ever have known. Then she remembered Miss Tuke saying that she thought the geologists were looking for somewhere to bury nuclear waste. Had they found the right kind of rock in which to bury their death canisters? Was this the evil that Sara feared was coming to the moor?

Suddenly Shantih stopped, her head lifted, her ears pricked sharply. The white stag was standing on an outcrop of rock on the hillside. It stood looking down on them with grace and majesty, pausing for a second before it raced away.

CHAPTER SEVEN

By the time Jinny reached Finmory Shantih was almost dry. When she had brought Bramble in and taken a dandy over him, she was able to start and groom Shantih. The dried sweat stung in her nostrils as she worked. Shantih could have broken a leg so easily, Jinny thought, shuddering. Once it had happened there was nothing she could have done.

'They've no right,' she swore, 'No right to fly their helicopter so low.'

Shantih's mane and tail shone under her body brush and her forelock was a wisp of silken hair on her precise, dished face. So easily she could have been injured, fatally injured. . .

'That will do you for to-day,' Jinny told them. 'Only the dress rehearsal. Posh you up proper for tomorrow night.'

When Jinny got in she tried to phone the police station at Ardtallon to tell them about the helicopter and ask if what the geologists had told her was true, but there was no reply.

In the kitchen Mrs Manders was peeling potatoes and Petra was perched on a corner of the table painting her nails.

'That helicopter buzzed us again,' Jinny told them, washing her hands. 'The pilot must be crazy. I'm telling you the hill was covered with deer. Hundreds! Well . . . a lot. He was just driving them where he wanted, and Shantih came down. I think someone should stop them. I phoned the police but there was no one there.'

'Is Shantih all right?' asked her mother. 'Did you hurt yourself?'

'She's okay. Luckily. Could have been killed,' said Jinny

'They can't be allowed to go on panicking the whole moor like that. Bet you Mr MacKenzie doesn't know they're doing it. No one on the moors to see them just now.'

'What were you doing up there then?' asked Petra examining her splayed fingers.

'Looking for the white stag,' muttered Jinny not wanting to talk about it but Petra had already lost interest and returned to the interrupted conversation she had been having with her mother.

'I can't possibly wear my blue dress. Lucy Fairfax is going to the party tonight and she's seen me in it.'

'And I saw the geologists. Up to no good. Told me I was trespassing!'

'Then wear your white dress and take your gold shawl.'

'Too posh,' said Petra. 'Especially my shawl. Need to be something really special before I wear that. I would never wear it to just an ordinary party! Do you think I could wear my black velvet skirt and top?'

'Go and try them on and let us see you.'

Petra went willingly.

'I don't know why you bother,' said Jinny sourly. 'In the end she'll wear exactly what she wants to wear. She doesn't care what you think.'

'It's all part of the fun, deciding what you'll wear. A new boy friend too, Dennis Laird.'

In minutes Petra was back. She was wearing a full black skirt, black high heeled shoes and a vivid, rainbow-striped top. Her necklace and earrings were flashing slivers of fluorescent metal. She whirled round in front of her mother. 'Well?' she asked.

Jinny watched from under drawn brows. 'Of course I'm not jealous,' she thought, 'It's just that she's so smug. So bloomin' pleased with herself all the time.'

'Your hair's sticking up at the back,' said Jinny and went to clean herself up a bit for the afternoon.

'Tell me about the play,' said Ken sitting easily astride Bramble, as they rode in to Glenbost for the dress rehearsal.

His legs were too long for the Highland but because he was hard and lean, he looked right on him.

'Mostly carols,' said Jinny. 'So everyone can join in. Angels. Mary can sing. You can't hear a word the shepherds say but Miss Broughton is working on them.'

She paused wanting to tell Ken how important it was that the nativity play should be something really tremendous, especially the kings: most especially of all the Golden King on Shantih.

'Wait till you see it today. Be super when we're all dressed up. Miss Broughton has made new wings for the angels and we've all to try on our costumes.'

In actual fact Jinny hadn't seen the king's costumes but riding beside Ken that didn't seem too important.

'Miss Tuke is the Silver King – her tunic is blue and grey; her cloak silver, embroidered with crystals; her boots are grey velvet and her silver crown is hung with icicles. She has a blue beard.

'Your costume is black. Black suedes and leathers; and your cloak is embroidered with jet and lined with purple satin so deep it's almost black and your crown is. . .'

'Black diamonds,' said Ken.

'With a single ruby,' said Jinny. 'A glowing heart of fire.'

'Amongst the flames,' said Ken.

'And I am the Golden King. My thigh boots are of orange-gold leather. My tunic is emblazoned with the sun and my cloak is pure gold, rolled out so finely that it is lighter than silk. My crown is studded with diamonds and nuggets of gold. Shantih is shod with gold and her mane and tail are braided with strands of gold.'

And Jinny saw how they had travelled the hard lands to

find the Child, following a star that blazed before them and stood at last above a stable doorway, brighter than a thousand suns.

'Joy,' she said. 'Tidings of great joy,' and Ken smiled his slow smile that lit up the green flecks in his eyes.

'Or something like that,' added Jinny, because with the turn of the road Glenbost with Miss Tuke's trailer parked by the field was in sight.

Miss Tuke had brought her dun Highland pony Guizer and to the accompaniment of his whinnyings they left Shantih and Bramble in the field.

In the church hall ten pairs of wings made from white cardboard pasted with tissues were carefully laid out on chairs. A donkey on wheels was abandoned beside them. In the space where the play would take place Mr Redding, Miss Tuke and Miss Broughton were opening tea chests. The children wriggled and squirmed to get a better view but stayed attached to their chairs.

'On the dot,' Mr Redding greeted them. 'Good to see you Ken. We're just opening the boxes. Come and help.'

'Good,' said Miss Broughton. 'That's a load off my mind. The angels' gowns are here,' and reaching into the tea chest she took out a pile of white folded sheets. When she held them up Jinny saw that each one had a hole cut in the centre for an angel's head.

'Debbie, come and get them,' Miss Broughton said and handed out the sheets to a girl with freckles and cropped black hair. 'Now there's different sizes so hold them up against each other until you've got them sorted out. And here's the halos.'

Miss Broughton dumped an entanglement of tinsel and hair grips on top of the sheets.

The shepherds' costumes were an assortment of dressing gowns, checked tea towels and head bands. Mary had a long, pale-blue gown and a white sheet with a blue head band. Joseph had a brown dressing gown and a piece of tweedy material for his head dress.

Jinny watched from a numbed distance. She could not believe that these tashed, rubbishy bits of clothing were meant to be costumes. They weren't even good enough for a nursery school dressing-up box.

From a second chest Mr Redding took out a battered wooden manger and a loose-limbed, sandy coloured dog with the stuffing leaking out of it.

'Is that everything?' he said.

'Do we wear anything?' asked Miss Tuke making the children giggle at the thought of a naked Miss Tuke.

'Ah yes, the kings,' said Mr Redding and plunged into the tea chest again.

He gave Ken a black toy sword, Miss Tuke a wooden dagger that had once been painted silver and to Jinny a sword with a steel blade.

'Looks utterly lethal,' he warned. 'Best keep it in its scabbard.'

Rooting into the tea chest again he brought out an armful of kings' costumes. Miss Tuke had a grey tabard made from an old army blanket, a leather belt and a piece of folkweave curtain to pin to her shoulders as her cloak. Ken had an old black shawl for his cloak, and two safety pins with which to pin it on.

Mr Redding held out Jinny's costume – a tabard made out of a yellow bath towel and a length of soiled, yellow hessian frayed at the edge into a fringe.

Jinny stared at the things in disgust. She looked up at Mr Redding's beaming face in dismay. 'Shall we try on the angels' wings?' he was asking, expecting Jinny to take her costume as all the others had done, but Jinny couldn't, knew that she should but couldn't.

'Costumes!' she cried her voice squeaking with disappointment. 'They're not costumes! They're nothing

64

but old rags. You can't have kings dressed up in bits of old curtain. Look at it! It's filthy!' and Jinny snatched the yellow hessian and held it up.

It looked as if at some time it had been used to cover a table or a notice board. You could still see where the nails had torn the cloth. From there it had gone down in life to being used as a paint rag or a floor cloth – stains and drips of dried paint textured its surface.

'I couldn't wear that. Shantih wouldn't be a golden horse if I was wearing that trash.'

'Oh dear,' said Mr Redding. 'Well these do seem to be the costumes that are always used.'

'Not this time!' shouted Jinny. 'I'm not wearing it. How will people see us as kings if we're dressed as beggars, Ken's is rubbish too and Miss Tuke's is just an ancient, old blanket. What's the use of doing it if we're not going to do it properly?' and she threw the hessian onto the floor.

'I'd no idea you felt so strongly about it,' said Mr Redding, his social worker beam fading from his face.

'Behave yourself, Jinny,' growled Miss Tuke, as if she were speaking to a pony that was mucking about with her. 'Enough of that rudeness.'

'I'm not wearing it,' blurted Jinny, aware of the children's watching faces, their prick-eared listening, the uneasy silence that filled the hall. 'And I'm not being a king if the others are wearing that rubbish.'

Jinny flipped back her long hair and stared defiantly at Mr Redding.

'Well now,' he said. 'Oh dear. . .'

'And that's that,' added Jinny. 'I think you should be ashamed of yourselves putting on a nativity play when you've no decent costumes!' and Jinny spun round and ran out of the hall.

Without stopping she tore down to the field, sprang over the gate, calling to Shantih.

'They're useless costumes,' she told Shantih as the Arab, sensing Jinny's distress, came high-stepping towards her. 'I'm not being a king if that's all there is for us to wear. We're going home.'

Jinny marched furiously into the shed to get Shantih's tack.

She reached up for Shantih's saddle and was about to lift it down when she stopped.

'Making a fool of yourself, Manders. You want Shantih to be the Golden Horse, don't you?' and Jinny knew she did. 'Ride away now and she won't be. You don't want that do you? So?'

Jinny groaned a camel-groan of despair. She would have to go back and apologize.

'You'll need to wait a bit longer,' she told Shantih and set off back to the hall.

'I'm sorry for losing my temper,' she said to Mr Redding, making sure that Miss Tuke and Miss Broughton could hear. 'But what I said is true. I'm not wearing that old hessian. I'll take all the costumes home and do them up a bit. And I'll find another cloak.'

Mr Redding beamed upon her. 'What a good idea,' he said. 'I must admit they are rather weary. We'll need to think about new ones for next year. If you could do something to brighten them up a bit that would be wonderful but do remember you've only got tonight. Tomorrow is the play.'

'Don't worry, I'll manage,' said Jinny, without the faintest idea what she was going to do to the costumes.

The rehearsal took longer than usual and when the kings rode up the path they rode into the glare of spotlights. Shantih, blinded by the savage light, spooked and shied until, to Jinny's shame, Amanda Bowen had to lead her up the path.

As Jinny carefully set down the box wrapped in tattered

Christmas paper before the new baby-doll Jesus and knelt in front of the manger, she felt a lump choking in her throat. She remembered the terror of the helicopter roaring behind her; the infectious panic of the deer; Shantih's crashing fall; the watching geologists and now the disaster of the costumes.

Jinny bit hard into her lower lip. She would find some way of making the kings look like kings. The nativity play must come alive for everyone. It must be good. Had to be the best possible play. People had to see her as the Golden King and Shantih dancing golden from the spotlights' glare.

CHAPTER EIGHT

Mrs Manders went into the box-room with Jinny and dragged out a trunk that was full of Granny Manders' things. On top there were photographs and ornaments that Jinny had almost forgotten, things that had been so familiar to her before Granny Manders had died. So strange that they should be here and Granny Manders dead, so dead that Jinny hardly ever thought about her. Once, all the ornaments must have been new – presents or things that Granny Manders had saved up to buy. Jinny picked up a metal tortoise and cradled it in the palm of her hand. Now no one knew the story behind it.

'Jinny!' exclaimed her mother. 'Stop daydreaming. I'm perfectly willing to help you but I am not doing everything.'

'Sorry,' muttered Jinny and hurriedly helped her mother take out bedspreads and curtains from the bottom of the trunk.

'Should get something out of these,' her mother said and they carried their spoils down to the kitchen table.

'I could make you all tunics out of this,' suggested Mrs Manders as she shook out a glistening bedspread of shimmering greens and peacock blues.

'All the same?'

'Well it's the best we've got. Certainly royal enough. You'll all have cloaks of your own colours?'

'I'll decorate them,' said Jinny. 'That would be smashing. Thank you very much.'

Jinny waited impatiently, getting in her mother's way as Mrs Manders measured and cut out three tunics.

'I know your size and Ken's and I've made Miss Tuke's ample,' she said as her sewing machine hummed along the material. 'You'll all be wearing them on top of your outdoor clothes won't you?'

Impatiently Jinny supposed they would.

As her mother finished the first tunic which was Ken's, Jinny thanked her, took it from her and ran upstairs with it. She had fabric paints that Mike had given to her on her last birthday. On Ken's tunic she would paint a black winter tree, the tracery of its branches covering the front of the tunic, on her own she would paint a yellow and orange sunburst and on Miss Tuke's a silver filigree of snowflake patterns.

Jinny pushed open the door of her room, her mind full of the paintings she was going to do. It was a fizzy feeling, knowing exactly how she was going to paint something, almost feeling the brush in her hands and yet until she had finished the painting nothing was certain.

She stepped under the arch into a drench of moonlight and felt the skin creep on her scalp, her flesh clutch tightly to her bones, for the room was full of the force of the Red Horse. Jinny stood in front of the painting and Sara's words rang in her mind. 'Only the red horse you ride can save,' and Jinny was certain that the white stag was in danger.

She ran to the window and staring out into the moonlight she saw the stag standing on the hill, its head turned towards Finmory House. As Jinny watched, it threw back its head and roared its challenge into the silent night.

For a moment longer Jinny clutched the costumes to her, standing stock still.

'Evil and greed threaten the white stag.' echoed Sara's voice. 'Only the red horse you ride can save,' and Jinny knew that she had no choice. The white stag needed her.

She had to go, had to tack up Shantih and ride out onto the moors, following where the white stag led.

Jinny threw the costumes onto her bed and went hurtling downstairs to the landing. Her heart pounding in her throat she raced along the corridor and plummeted straight into her father's arms.

'Steady,' he warned. 'What's the hurry?'

'Nothing,' mumbled Jinny. 'I've just got to go down and see Shantih.'

'You don't look as if there's any "just" about it. You look as if it's an emergency,' and Mr Manders turned his daughter to face a mirror that was on the wall.

Jinny caught a glimpse of herself – eyes staring from her head, mouth clenched shut, her hair wild – then twisting free from her father's hand on her shoulder, she raced on.

'Come back,' commanded her father.

'Don't stop,' Jinny told herself. 'Keep running. If you go back he'll stop you riding to the stag. He won't let you go out onto the moors at night.'

'Jinny,' warned her father. 'Come back.'

On the top step of the stairs going down to the hall, Jinny stopped. When her father spoke in that tone of voice there was nothing else she could do except obey.

'Please,' she pleaded desperately. 'I must get Shantih and go and find the white stag. I saw it from the window. It needs help. I must ride out and find it. Please. I must.'

'You mean it has hurt itself?'

'Sort of,' said Jinny, knowing it would be no use trying to explain to her father about Sara's fears for the stag, her warning of evil stalking the moors.

'Then let's have another look out of your window, though I really don't see what we could do if it has hurt itself.'

Mr Manders led the way back to Jinny's room with Jinny following reluctantly behind him.

'There's nothing there now,' he stated as they both stared out at the desolate hillside.

'But the white stag was there,' insisted Jinny. 'I know it needed help. Please let me go out and find it. I'll be safe on Shantih!'

'If the stag was there it's not there now, so it can't be badly hurt, not when it has made off in a few minutes. I'm quite sure you don't need to worry about it.'

'But I do. I am worried about it. Desperately worried.'

'I thought you were so worried about your play? Your mother's worked all evening making the costumes. I thought you were going to decorate them?'

'I will afterwards. Honestly I will,' said Jinny wildly.

'Jinny, listen to me. You are not to ride over the moors tonight. You know how dangerous it is. I absolutely forbid it. Promise me you won't.'

And Jinny knew there was no way she could disobey her father.

'Promise,' she mumbled, too defeated to even bother crossing her fingers.

'Good,' said her father. 'Were you up here for your paints?'

Jinny nodded.

'Then find them and bring everything you need down to the kitchen. Far too cold up here.'

'So he can keep an eye on me,' Jinny thought, scrabbling in her cupboard for paints and brushes.

Before she followed her father back downstairs she took a last careful look out over the moors, but there was no sign of the stag. Had it been nothing more than her imagination? And yet she knew that it had been more than that. The white stag had needed her and she had failed it.

When Jinny had finished painting the tunics Ken came in with three crowns made from intricate twistings of wire.

'They need jewels,' said Jinny, trying hers on, feeling it lifting above her head, making her walk taller and straighter.

'Nice,' Ken said of Jinny's painted tunics. 'But not enough. They should be encrusted, textured, voluptuous.'

'I know,' said Jinny.

Mrs Manders had made a black cloak for Ken from one of Granny Manders' evening dresses and sewn ruffles of silver onto Miss Tuke's folkweave curtain.

'Can't find anything golden for you,' she said to Jinny. 'Wonder what we could think up?'

'There's that shop in Inverburgh,' said Jinny. 'If I'd known sooner I could have gone in there and looked for stuff. They've glass jewels and braids, super wools and glitzy remnants.'

With the air of a magician Ken took a five pound note from his pocket.

'Glitter for the kings,' he said giving it to Jinny, and her mother said the car was going into Inverburgh tomorrow morning. Jinny's eyes sparkled. Five pounds to spend on glitter! There might even be enough to buy gold stickers for Shantih's bridle.

'Thanks very much,' she said. 'Super.'

'Perhaps you'll find a remnant that would make you a cloak, or a trimming of some kind to jazz up that yellow material,' Mrs Manders said, but Jinny knew that there wasn't a chance: a hundred pounds would hardly buy the kind of cloak that the Golden King should wear in Jinny's nativity play.

'Anyway, that's all I can do for you tonight,' continued her mother. 'Must get some mince pies baked,' and she began to put away her sewing machine.

'They are absolutely smashing!' exclaimed Jinny gathering up cloaks, tunics and paints. 'I'm overflowing with thanks,' and she went back up to her room.

She stood uncertainly ouside her door, swallowed hard and went in. The air was silent; the Red Horse only a painting. She looked out of the window and the moors stretched moon-silver, silent, undisturbed as she had known they would.

'Only the red horse you ride can save.'

'It wasn't my fault,' Jinny defended herself. 'I was coming if Dad hadn't pounced. Honestly I was.'

But in her mind the ghost of Sara's voice murmured its warning of greed and evil.

Suddenly Jinny remembered that she hadn't gone down to say goodnight to the horses, hadn't seen Shantih since she had ridden home from the rehearsal and Ken had offered to see to Bramble and Shantih, letting Jinny get on with the costumes.

For a second Jinny hesitated. It was late and Shantih would be perfectly all right until tomorrow morning. She didn't really need to go and see her. Silly to think that Shantih would know whether she had been down to see her or not.

Beneath the good reasons there was the real reason: she had failed Sara and the Red Horse and she was afraid.

'Course I'm not,' Jinny told herself severely.

She went downstairs, put on her duffle, and wrapped her school scarf round her head and shouted to her parents that she was going out to see Shantih.

'Nothing more. Just to see her. Promise.'

Jinny shut the door and gritting her teeth she walked into the enchanted, moon-bright world. As she walked down to the stables she counted her footsteps, the numbers linking into a chain that held her to the safety of the house.

Jinny picked up the powerful torch they kept just inside the stable doorway. In its beam Bramble was a giant stuffed toy, curled in the straw. But Shantih stood with her chest straining against her half door, her neck arching over it, her great eyes staring from her face, the pits of her wide nostrils scarlet and her bed soiled and trampled, her rugs hanging to the floor.

'Whoa, the horse,' Jinny murmured in dismay. 'Steady now, what's wrong?' and she crossed quickly to her horse then saw to her astonishment that Shantih was soaking with sweat as if she had just come back from a fierce ride.

'Witch ridden,' thought Jinny and felt the shadows take forms about her. 'Stop it,' she warned herself. 'Don't start,' and she went into the box, took off the rugs, twisted a straw wisp and began to rub Shantih down, talking low and gentle to her as she worked.

'What happened to you?' Jinny whispered. 'What upset you?' but really she didn't need to ask. She knew that Shantih had heard the white stag, been aware of its presence and had been trying to join it on the moors.

At last when Shantih was dry again and her bed squared up, Jinny left her. Shutting the stable door she stood staring up towards Finmory. By the tack room wall Jinny was aware of a deeper darkness in the moon shadows. Someone was there. Tam? Sara? Jinny didn't wait to find out. She took to her heels and ran for home. No running steps followed her, no shadow waited for her.

'Nothing,' thought Jinny scornfully as the lighted kitchen welcomed her in. 'Running away from nothing!'

'I was just coming down to look for you,' said her father, the only one of her family left up. 'Make sure the kitchen light is off before you go to bed. And don't waste time mooning around here. If you're coming to Inverburgh with me tomorrow you'll need to be up sharpish.'

Coming in from a world of moon-haunting shades Jinny could only blink her agreement.

'Goodnight, then,' said her father. 'Sleep well.'

'Goodnight. And you,' said Jinny.

When her father's footsteps were lost in silence Jinny made herself a mug of chocolate and sat down at the table wrapping her hands round the mug for comfort. Whatever had happened on the moors that night the white stag had needed her and she hadn't been there. It wasn't only Sara's voice in her head, Shantih had known too.

Jinny sipped her chocolate and then went slowly upstairs. As she walked along the corridor she stopped outside Petra's empty bedroom door. Turning the knob with both hands she let herself in and slid the door shut behind her, stood for a second in the perfumed dark then switched on the light. Petra's pink and white bedroom was as perfect as a room in a show house. It always fascinated Jinny. There was literally not a thing out of place. She stared in disgusted amazement at the neat pile of fashion magazines, the bottles and jars in precisely the correct places on Petra's dressing table and her frilly, high heeled slippers by the side of her bed.

'We're not sisters,' Jinny thought. 'I'm a foundling,' but before her imagination could lure her into the delightful byways of who she really was, Jinny remembered Petra's golden shawl. She knew exactly where Petra kept it – wrapped in tissue paper in the bottom drawer of her dressing table.

'I'll only look at it,' Jinny told herself. 'It won't do any harm to just look at it.'

Jinny opened the drawer, pushed back the neat layers of folded sweaters and took out the long, flat folding of tissue paper. She crouched down on the floor and opened t to reveal Petra's shawl.

'Put it back. You've no right to touch it,' Jinny thought. But she didn't. She took it out of its tissue paper and holding it to her shoulders she posed in front of Petra's mirror.

'Must see what it looks like when I'm wearing my tunic and my crown,' Jinny thought and checking carefully to make sure that she hadn't left any telltale signs behind her, Jinny put the shawl back into its tissue paper and took it up to her room.

There, in the comfortable clutter of books, drawings, shoes and clothes, Jinny dressed in her costume, settled the crown on her head and held the shawl to her shoulders again. As she moved about, the shawl floated out in a golden sheening.

Jinny knew that never in a hundred million years would Petra let her borrow her shawl. She wouldn't even lend it to her for a royal garden party, let alone to be a cloak for a king. But it would be smashing.

'If I did borrow it,' Jinny thought, 'Petra need never know.'

Tonight she was staying with a school friend. She was not coming to the nativity play and when the play was over Jinny could find some way of putting it back into Petra's drawer. If her parents came to the play, her father would never notice that the golden king's cloak was Petra's shawl and her mother wouldn't tell on her. Petra need never know.

'Say it was torn or mucked up?' Jinny thought. 'Perhaps I'd better take it back.'

But Jinny didn't. She folded the shawl back into its tissue paper wrappings and hid it in her cupboard. It would be just right for the golden king.

CHAPTER NINE

Jinny's night was tormented by dreams. She galloped Shantih over a desolation of cinders, the geologists swinging their choppers, pursued her with the thunderous noise of the helicopter, or she was wandering alone in a mist, dressed in rags when she should have been a king and all around her Sara's voice cried out in distress.

Although she had spent most of the night tossing and turning, more awake than asleep, her mother had to wake her, telling her it was half past seven and if she didn't get up she would be too late to go into Inverburgh with them.

'It's all happening too soon, too quickly,' Jinny thought as she washed and dressed. 'It can't be the play tonight, Christmas Day tomorrow. I'm not ready for it. It's all too sudden.'

She dashed down to the stable, feeling the air less bitter than it had been. The sky was low slung with massed clouds. The wind had changed.

While Shantih and Bramble were feeding, Jinny mucked out around them.

'Tonight,' she told Shantih, strapping on her New Zealand rug and putting on her halter, 'You will be a king's horse in the best ever nativity play. They will all see how wonderful you are.'

When she led Shantih outside the Arab pranced at her side. Her head was high as she searched the moor and sent her call bannering over the hills, her ears tense for an answer.

'Forget it,' said Jinny sharply. 'You heard nothing last night. Nothing! You were only sweating because the weather had changed.'

'Witch ridden, hag ridden,' whispered Jinny's imagination but she refused to listen. Grabbing Bramble's forelock she urged both horses on to their field.

Turned loose, Bramble started to graze at once but even when Jinny came back with their hay Shantih was still hightailing it round the field, only stopping to whinny and listen for an answer from the reaching moors.

'Stop it!' screamed Jinny uselessly. 'Stop it, idiot horse! You've to be a king's horse tonight so bloomin' behave yourself.'

Shantih came over to her hay, picking at it in mouthfuls, chewing it with her head up, listening. Jinny stood and stared, lost in admiration for the beauty of her horse – the carved line of her head against the grey sky, the cascading fall of her mane.

'If Dad hadn't caught me I would have ridden you out last night. I would, honestly I would.'

'Jinny!' yelled her father's voice. 'Jinny, come on.'

Sitting in the car behind her parents Jinny ate cold toast.

'High as a kite,' she thought. 'That's what I am.'

Her mind was an electronic excitement, whirling faster and faster – from Sara's voice to Petra's, from the thought of the nativity play happening in a few hours time to the distress of the deer fleeing from the helicopter.

'And I never phoned the police again,' Jinny thought desperately.

'Now we haven't much time,' said her father, when they had at last found a place to park. 'We've all to be back here in two hours. Jinny, is your watch going?'

Jinny checked, gave it a few quick winds in case it had been about to stop, for her watch was capricious, like time itself, not to be trusted.

'I've three more presents to find and food,' said Mrs Manders.

'And I've to go to the store to check up on how many more pots they want for the January sales,' said Mr Manders. 'Jinny?'

'Only the remnant shop, I think.'

'Then we meet back here at twelve on the dot. Right?'

Jinny slammed the car door behind her and ran into the busy Inverburgh streets. Last minute shoppers jostled and pushed, greed spangling from their eyes as they clutched crying toddlers, slapping at random or shouting at older children to hurry up. As Jinny fought her way through the crowds their voices of irritation and temper clawed at her ears. In the doorway of one of the big shops a Father Christmas clanged his bell and guffawed his false tinsel laughter.

'It shouldn't be like this,' Jinny thought. 'All this wanting, all this grabbing. This isn't the way it should be. If you gave the Child the most expensive gift you could buy it would be worth nothing,' and clearly Jinny saw how her headmaster was right. It had to be a gift from your inner self, from your heart. Something that cost you. The very best. Not something you just paid money for. He was right, a true gift would be to look at something, something you were afraid of, and accept it.

She smelt the butcher's before she reached it, the blood smell stronger than the traffic fumes. The shop was glass fronted, pink tiles on ceiling, walls and floor, a glass counter with sliced meat displayed inside it. Carcases hung from chrome spikes, paper frills decorated the stumps of their necks and the shop assistants wore white overalls and white caps. A queue of people filled the shop, garishly lit by the neon lighting. As the queue moved up they rubbed against the yellow fat and red flesh of the skinned carcases so that they seemed to dance.

This year Jinny's Christmas cards had been of a manger surrounded by worshipping animals – sheep, lambs and cattle. The same animals that hung here from their hooks. Jinny hated the thought of animals being slaughtered. All animals should be free to lead their own lives, as free as the deer living wild on the moors. Jinny caught sight of a pig's head sitting in front of the window. She swung away from it and in an instant was back amongst the jostling crowds, all thought of the butchers cancelled from her brain. She could not bear to think about it.

Jinny trotted down two wrong streets before she found her way to the remnant shop. Usually it was fairly empty but today it was busy with people looking for last minute gifts, so that Jinny had to dodge and pry, trying to decide what she would buy.

'I'm not shoplifting,' she explained to a suspicious assistant. 'I'm collecting.'

In the end she chose purple, silver and gold foil to wrap round the gift boxes, glass jewels for the crowns and a length of luminous plastic to make belts for their swords.

'Four pounds seventy six,' said the girl.

'Just made it,' said Jinny laying Ken's five pound note on the counter.

At the side of the counter was a wicker basket of fake jewellery. Waiting for her change Jinny picked out two gold brooches. They were just what she needed to pin Petra's shawl to her shoulders.

'Only fifty pence each,' said the girl.

'I'll take them,' said Jinny, not thinking before she spoke but saying the words because she so desperately wanted to wear Petra's shawl as her cloak, and to pay a pound for the brooches meant she was really going to do it. There would be no question now of putting the shawl back into Petra's drawer.

Jinny was ten minutes late getting back to the car.

'Another five minutes and I really would have gone without you,' said her father, but he was smiling so Jinny knew that the store must have sold a lot of his pottery and was wanting more for the sale.

'Went in to a bookshop,' she admitted.

'Did you get your costume things?' asked her mother.

'Oodles,' said Jinny opening the bag, spilling the jewels onto the car seat, taking care not to let her mother see the brooches.

They crawled out of the carpark into a jam of traffic which inched and stopped, inched and stopped its way along Inverburgh High street.

'Nip out and get a local paper,' said Mr Manders seeing a news vendor. 'I forgot to get one.'

Jinny nipped out, bought a paper and had only to walk a few steps to catch up with the car.

'Could be here all flipping day,' grumbled Mr Manders and her mother wondered aloud whether she had enough food to last them over Christmas. Jinny sat back, leafing through the paper, her eyes skimming the usual photographs of weddings, dances and coffee mornings. There was a double spread about Inverburgh shops – the store that bought her father's pottery, dress shops, grocers, the pink-tiled butchers and a page of hotels advertising Festive Fayre.

'I'll finish off the costumes whenever I get in and then groom Shantih,' Jinny thought, turning another page.

The shock of the photograph shot through her as if she had touched an electric fence. For a split second she could not help seeing it.

It showed a tumbled pile of dead red deer. Creatures of such grace and beauty reduced to a pile of carcases. The shock was too sudden, the killing too impossible. With twitching fingers Jinny shut the paper and thrust it down. Shuddering she wrapped her arms round herself. Their car, her parents, were no longer enough to keep her safe.

'No!' she thought. 'No!' and shut it out of her mind.

Leaning over the back of her mother's seat she gabbled on about the nativity play.

'We'll need to leave about ten,' she said. 'Miss Tuke's coming to put on her costume and then drive on with Guizer to Glenbost. I expect she'll want coffee. Better have something ready for her anyway, but don't let her settle and do NOT offer her a drink or she'll never reach Glenbost. End up in a ditch if she starts boozing.'

'Miss Tuke?' said her mother.

'Oh yes,' said Jinny. 'I've seen her knocking back the whisky.'

It wasn't true but Jinny didn't care. She only wanted noise to blot out the dead deer, to unhook from behind her eyes the detail of a nostril dripping blood that was fixed there like a burr and wouldn't go away.

When they got back Ken had painted the crowns – purple, silver and gold. When the jewels were fixed in place with fuse wire, they were glittering, fantastic creations.

'Hope you don't have to gallop too far wearing those,' said Mr Manders.

Petra, returning, was so full of the news that she had been invited to a bigger, posher party that night that she hardly noticed the crowns and when Jinny pointed them out to her she only said, with Infant Mistress condescension, 'Bit home made but I don't suppose anyone in Glenbost will care.'

Now that Petra was back Jinny was uneasily aware of her sister's every movement. If she was not actually in the same room as Jinny it meant that she might be in her bedroom looking for her shawl.

'Put it back,' urged Jinny's conscience. 'Even if she catches you with it you can always say you were just looking at it.'

'I can't,' swore Jinny. 'I must have it as my cloak. MUST.'

Jinny followed her sister into the front room. Paper chains and lanterns hung from the ceiling, holly clustered around mirrors and picture frames. The Christmas tree stood at the window bearing its strange artificial fruit of baubles and fairy lights and round its base the temptation of unopened presents. Christmas cards were hung around the walls and crowded mantelpiece and cabinet.

By this time tomorrow they would all be here pulling crackers, opening presents, too full of Christmas dinner to eat chocolates or nuts. But this year for Jinny was not like any other Christmas. Normally there was nothing else to do but get ready for the day, but this year there were so many things still to happen before Jinny could even begin to think of presents or Christmas dinner.

Sara's voice still echoed in her mind. Jinny knew that she had failed the white stag. It was too late to do anything about it now. Her guilt was like a dentist's drill on an exposed nerve.

'Why don't you ask her if you can borrow it,' suggested Jinny's conscience changing channels.

'She'd only say, "no" and go and make sure that I hadn't taken it.'

Petra was writing a note to say thank you for the party and how much she'd enjoyed it.

'To make sure they'll ask her next year,' Jinny thought and twisting herself into weird shapes she did silent Monty Python silly walks behind her sister's back.

'Oh here you are, Jinny,' said her mother. 'Isn't it time you were bringing Shantih and Bramble in?'

'Just going to,' said Jinny, pretending to be scratching her head not making clawing gestures over Petra.

In the kitchen her father was reading the local paper. Jinny went past him warily, looking the other way in case she should see the photograph of the dead deer.

Ken came down to groom Bramble and Jinny hung the

torch from a beam between the two boxes. They worked in silence, only their whispering speech to their horses, the rasp of dandy on fetlock and tail, the sweep of body brush and the hollow clomp of hooves as they moved the horses over disturbed the stillness. The torchlight glazed Shantih's eyes, sent dazzling silver pathways flowing from the sweep of the body brush as Jinny leant her weight against hard neck, muscled shoulder, rounded barrel and over the gleaming mass of Shantih's quarters.

'In a stable,' thought Jinny and Betjeman's lines came into her head, "The Maker of the stars and sea, Become a Child on earth for me?"

'Do you believe it?' she said to Ken her voice urgent, uncertain. 'Really believe it happened?'

'Yes,' said Ken.

'That a baby was really God?'

'Hear beyond the ear, see beyond the eye,' said Ken. 'Beyond the understanding of the mind. Yes.'

Jinny felt the stable shimmer with the light she had seen in the church hall during the first rehearsal. Was there and was gone and she was worrying about Petra again.

When they had finished grooming, Bramble's heavy coat shone in single lustrous hairs, his mane and winter-wide tail were subdued, his muzzle was pile velvet and Shantih was svelte, sophisticated, alien. Ken and Jinny left them pulling at their hay nets and went back to the house.

'You've been ages,' judged Petra which meant that she hadn't discovered her shawl was missing.

'When are you going to your party?' Jinny asked.

'Oh not until ten,' said Petra making Jinny's heart drop. 'We've to be at Tulah's about eleven. Actually it's her parents' do. They're having a dinner first, then we're joining in. Dennis is coming for me.'

'Boring,' said Jinny. 'Sounds v. boring to me,' and at

once she wished she hadn't. She did not want to rouse Petra.

'Typical. If it's not horses it's boring. Time you grew out of it.'

'Shan't,' snapped Jinny and went up to her room to bring down Miss Tuke's costume so that it would be ready for her when she arrived.

Jinny stood looking at the two costumes – her own and Miss Tuke's – spread out on the bed, imagining Miss Tuke's green wellies under the silken tunic and the tasselled cloak.

Jinny took the shawl out of her cupboard, found the two brooches she had bought and shaking out the gold silk of the shawl, she folded it in half and pinned it to her shoulders.

Jinny moved in front of her wardrobe mirror; even in cords and sweater the shawl transformed her. It was not really the cloak that she had dreamed of – the cloak of pure gold – but it was enough. She set the jewelled crown on her head.

'Born a King on Bethlehem's plain
Gold I bring to crown him again
King forever, ceasing never
Over us all to reign.'

Jinny sang silently, in to herself, so that her out-of-tune singing wouldn't spoil it. She felt Shantih trot in exultation to the open doors of the church hall. She heard the audience's gasp of surprised delight when they saw the Golden King on his flaunting magical steed. They would remember this play forever.

'Jinny!' yelled Petra's voice. 'You've got my shawl, haven't you? You little beast! You have got it!'

Petra's footsteps raged along the landing, beat a furious tattoo up the stairs to Jinny's room, where Jinny stood petrified, staring at her ridiculous reflection in the mirror.

CHAPTER TEN

For a second the sisters confronted each other. Petra's neat face disarranged by rage, Jinny's face like a mask.

'Get it off,' stormed Petra. 'Get if off at once. You nasty, thieving little prowler, Going into my room, taking my things! Give it back to me.'

'No,' said Jinny. 'You don't need it. You're not going to wear it. You said it was too good for the party.'

'Give it back to me!' screamed Petra. 'It's mine.'

'But you don't need it and I do. I MUST have a cloak to wear tonight.'

'Don't talk such nonsense. Who cares what you wear in your silly little church play. As if it makes any difference. Now give it to me.'

'No!'

'Oh yes you will,' cried Petra and she threw herself at Jinny trying to unfasten the brooches that held her shawl to Jinny's shoulders.

'Get off!' screamed Jinny. 'Leave me alone,' and she pushed Petra away from her.

'I'm having it back,' Petra shouted and suddenly Jinny was no longer just pushing her sister away she was fighting her for possession of the shawl. Her hands tore at Petra's hair, her legs and feet grappled against her as they swung from side to side yelling insults at each other. Then Jinny's foot caught against Petra's ankle. She felt herself falling and, grabbing at Petra she pulled her down with her. They hit the floor with a crash and rolled over, fighting furiously.

'Girls!' roared Mrs Manders' voice from somewhere

above them. Jinny hadn't even heard her mother come in. 'Stop this at once! This minute! I never saw such an exhibition. Get up!'

Somehow Jinny disentangled herself from Petra and scrambled to her feet.

'She took my shawl,' said Petra justifying herself as she stood up. 'And she won't give it back to me. I was trying to. . .'

'Two young women fighting like that. I'm ashamed of you both, I really am. Jinny give the shawl back to Petra at once.'

Jinny undid the brooches and with a leaden sense of doom handed the shawl to her sister.

'Thanks,' said Petra sarcastically, snatching it from her. 'And don't you dare go snooping round my room again.'

'You'd no right to take it,' said Mrs Manders. 'I suppose you wanted it for your play tonight?'

Jinny nodded, a lump in her throat choking her. 'Don't let her see you crying,' she told herself furiously as she felt her eyes filling with tears.

'Why didn't you ask Petra if you could borrow it?'

'No point,' said Jinny her voice shaking. 'You know she'd never have let me have it.'

'Are you wearing it tonight?' Mrs Manders asked Petra.

'That's beside the point,' said Petra. 'You don't think I'd lend it to her now, not after she's stolen it,' and shaking out her shawl, folding it neatly, she turned to go.

'I'll have to wear that rubbishy bit of hessian,' Jinny thought, knowing it was too late to try to find anything else. In half an hour Miss Tuke would have arrived.

'Please let me borrow it?' said Jinny despising herself for asking.

'No,' said Petra and marched back to her bedroom.

Jinny picked up the crown from where it had fallen and sat on her bed trying to straighten out the wire, seeing it through a haze of tears.

'You really shouldn't have touched it,' said her mother. 'You know what she's like about her things.'

And Jinny was crying – great gulping sobs that tore the heart out of her.

'Oh don't Jinny, don't. It's not as important as all that. Can't we tack some tinsel round the yellow material?'

'It's not for me,' blurted Jinny, trying to explain. 'It's for Shantih so she can be a golden horse, for the audience, so that it will be the best ever nativity play. I do so want it to be the best.'

'Come on,' said her mother. 'Mop up. You can't be a king if your face is all swollen. Come and see what I can find.'

Jinny wiped her face and reluctantly followed her mother downstairs to her bedroom.

'Made a fool of myself again,' she thought, feeling utterly forlorn as she watched her mother taking down a flat dress-box from the top of a cupboard. Jinny knew it contained her mother's wedding dress but she couldn't think how that could be any use.

Her mother put the box on the bed, opened it, took out her wedding dress and laid it on the bed. She lifted the brown tissue paper that had been underneath the dress and revealed a shimmering of gold. She took it out of the box, shook it and held it out to Jinny.

'How would that do?' she asked.

Jinny stared in disbelief, for the evening cloak her mother was holding up did not seem to be made of material but of shimmering gold, truly as if it had been made from beaten gold.

'It's gold lamé,' explained Mrs Manders. 'Originally it belonged to my grandmother. She gave it to me and I had it remodelled. I've hardly worn it since I've been married.'

'But it's far too good. I couldn't take it.'

'You're right,' agreed Mrs Manders, laughing. 'That's why I didn't mention it before. But you can have it for tonight.'

'You really mean it?' demanded Jinny.

Her mother nodded.

'Oh it is frabjous, super, super. Thank you so much,' and Jinny threw her arms round her mother's neck in total gratitude.

'Take care of it,' warned Mrs Manders when at last Jinny released her. 'I wore it to a ball once.'

'With Dad?'

'No, long before I met him.'

'Thank you! Thank you!' chanted Jinny as she went racing back to her room with the cloak. When she tried it on, it fell from her shoulders to below her knees in falls of gold. Perfection.

Splashing her face with cold water so that no one else should know she had been crying Jinny heard Miss Tuke arrive.

'Snow-o, snow-o,' she announced cheerfully. 'Old Biddy's shaking her goose feathers at us,' and she went with Mr Manders through to the front room, seeing it was Christmas, to accept the sherry he had offered her.

Jinny gathered up Miss Tuke's costume and took it down to her.

'Well now!' exclaimed Miss Tuke. 'Someone's been busy,' and she put on the tunic, belted the sword about her middle and set the crown on her head.

'Frankincense to offer have I
Incense owns a deity nigh. . . '

boomed Miss Tuke, strutting round the room, her crown slightly askew, her cherry nose scarlet from the cold and her sherry glass in her hand.

'Look more like St Nick to me' said Mr Manders.

'But I haven't got it. No frankincense.'

'Forgot the gifts,' cried Jinny and dived back upstairs.

On her bed the sight of the gold lamé cloak sent shivers of delight sparkling through her. She spread her open hands in front of it. She could hardly believe it was possible, suspected that it might be fairy gold ready to vanish before her eyes.

Kneeling on the floor, Jinny wrapped silver foil round the box that was Miss Tuke's gift, gold foil round her own and purple foil round the box that was to be Ken's, but it did not matter how much she decorated them, they were nothing but empty boxes, gifts of nothing to be offered to the Child. Her headmaster would not approve.

Yet it was not only her headmaster who would no approve. It was Jinny herself. She had to find something real to offer to the infant Jesus. If she had only been wearing the tashed hessian, the gaudy box would have been enough but now she was wearing the cloak of gold she needed a gift of consciousness. She must force herself to look at something of which she was afraid. The starving humans whose gaunt presence haunted their Christmas feasting? The mass slaughter of the creatures who had knelt in the stable?

'Jinny,' called her father. 'Are you knitting it?'

'Coming,' Jinny yelled and hurtled downstairs, grateful for her father's interruption.

'May as well take all the costumes with me?' suggested Miss Tuke. 'We can all garb up together when we get there.'

'Good idea,' said Mrs Manders and went to get a case for the costumes.

With the case on the floor beside her, the crowns and gifts on the seat next to her, Miss Tuke revved up her engine.

'Nearly time you two were on the move,' she told Ken and Jinny before she drove off. 'I'm early to help tie on wings and things but we don't want to keep the Rev hanging about.'

Jinny pulled on an extra yellow sweater to wear under her costume, tied a scarf round her head to wear under her hard hat and buttoned up her duffle. She waited for Ken in the kitchen. The local paper lay folded where her father had left it.

'Take the photograph of the deer and look at it. You're afraid of it. To look at it would be a present for the Child.'

Jinny's mind shied violently away from the thought. It was a stupid idea that would only upset her. But Jinny knew that was how Petra looked at things. Petra who wouldn't even lend Jinny her miserable shawl.

'If it's a stupid thought and you're not afraid of it, look at it now,' Jinny challenged herself.

But she couldn't. Garish in her mind's eye she saw the blood drip from the dead nostril, the glazed eyes and the slack, lifeless fall of the deer's legs.

'Go on. Look at it.'

'But it's Christmas,' Jinny protested. 'Everyone's meant to be happy at Christmas. You're not meant to go getting upset about things at Christmas.'

Maybe Christmas is meant to be a time when things are upset, thought Jinny suddenly. Not an easy time. Not easy for the kings, travelling on and on; not easy for Mary having a baby in an outhouse; not easy for Joseph knowing the baby wasn't his or for the shepherds, maybe the angels had only been in their minds and yet they had obeyed them. None of it easy. The Baby to cause more upset than anything else, ever.

91

'We'll be there,' said Mrs Manders coming into the kitchen to find Jinny staring into space.

'What?' demanded Jinny coming back to Finmory kitchen with a start.

'I'm only saying Dad and I will be there to cheer you on. Mike is definitely not coming but we'll be there.'

'Great,' said Jinny. 'You'll see Shantih. And your cloak.'

As Jinny followed Ken's angular, black shape down through the garden, clouds were massed beyond the sea but the sky was clear and the pock-eyed moon rode high.

'It will shine cold radiance on my cloak,' thought Jinny. 'And on my gift of gold.'

'Some gift,' mocked the voice in Jinny's head. 'An empty box!'

Jinny stood still, racked by indecision, by not wanting to do what she knew she was going to do.

'Wait,' she shouted to Ken. 'I've forgotten something.'

She raced back to the kitchen where the paper waited. Knowing the right sheet by the advertisments on the back of the photograph, Jinny tore it out and folding it she crammed it into her pocket.

'There,' she told herself. 'I've got it, so shut up,' and she raced out after Ken.

Shantih and Bramble startled to their box doors and stared in amazement when they saw their tack.

'Different, I know,' soothed Jinny trying to reach up to Shantih's head to fasten her throatlash. 'But this is Christmas Eve. You can't expect things to be everyday ordinary.'

Bramble glowered, ears pinned back, nostrils mean and wrinkled. He snapped at Ken, blowing himself out to full balloon size trying to stop Ken tightening his girths.

Outside in the yard Ken swung himself effortlessly into the saddle but each time Jinny lifted her foot to the stirrup

Shantih skittered away leaving Jinny hopping madly or grounded.

'Stand still you idiot,' Jinny shouted, trying to make her voice dominant, in control, when all the time she could only think how magnificent Shantih looked, spirited and powerful, neck crested, back high, defiant against this night riding.

In the end Jinny sprang onto Shantih and felt her horse rear almost before she was in the saddle. But Jinny loved her for it. Loved her as she led the way, volatile, high-stepping towards Mr MacKenzie's, Bramble's hoofbeats clopping behind her.

Jinny had lost all track of time, could not think how late it was.

'The MacKenzie's must be coming,' Jinny called back to Ken as she passed the lighted farmhouse and wondered what Mr MacKenzie's sober-black, Bible-carrying, Sunday self would think about having horses almost in the church.

Guiltily Jinny saw that there were lights on in the bothy too. Glancing quickly up the hill she saw that there were figures of tinkers silhouetted against the light.

As they rode past the farm and out onto the Glenbost road, Sara was standing a little way back from the roadside. For a second Jinny thought she was only a shadow, then her pale face, almost luminous in the green-silver moonlight, turned to look straight at her.

Drowning in guilt Jinny tried to stop Shantih, to shout to Sara that her father had forbidden her to ride after the white stag, that it hadn't been her fault; but Shantih plunged to follow Bramble carrying Jinny away from Sara.

'Behave yourself you idiot,' Jinny muttered, fighting her horse, trying furiously to turn Shantih back.

'I couldn't . . .' began Jinny.

'Tonight is the ceremony of the Christ Child,' said Sara in a low, clear voice. 'You are called to be there. Ride your red horse.'

Before Jinny could reply, Shantih had dragged the reins through her hands and was galloping after Bramble.

'What did she say?' asked Ken.

'Don't know,' said Jinny not wanting to discuss it, and she banished all thoughts of the tinkers from her head. Thinking only of the nativity play, she closed her legs on Shantih's sides and sent her on to Glenbost.

Ken caught up with her and they trotted side by side, only twice dropping into single file – once when a car passed them going to Finmory and the second time when it passed them again with Petra sitting in the passenger seat.

'I'll bet she's not wearing her rotten shawl,' Jinny thought, ignoring her sister.

Glenbost came into sight and nearly all the houses had lighted windows. The church and church hall were ablaze with spotlights. Nothing was left in Jinny's head except the play: that it should be the very best.

As they reached the path that led up to the church, a van came speeding towards them, making Shantih rear forward and Bramble plunge up the banking at the side of the path.

The tadpole geologist was at the wheel. He swung the huge van round in a vicious U-turn and roared back towards the village.

'That is the last we will be seeing of them,' said a woman clutching an angel by the hand, who like Bramble, had taken refuge on the banking. 'Heathen it is to be leaving a place on Christmas Eve.'

Trotting up the path to the church hall, Jinny paid no attention to the woman. The next time she rode Shantih through the glare of the spotlights she would be the Golden King riding her horse of fire.

She had totally forgotten the photograph crushed in her pocket.

CHAPTER ELEVEN

Miss Tuke's car and trailer were parked by the side of the field and Guizer's thunderous whinnyings and crashing hooves followed Ken and Jinny as they rode up to the church hall.

'Better go and find Tukey before he smashes up the trailer,' said Jinny jumping down from Shantih and giving her reins to Ken.

Miss Tuke was in the small kitchen off the hall, elbow deep in sheeted angels and shepherds in dressing gowns. Miss Broughton was handing out lambs and crooks while Mary sat by the cooker, her face as white as her headress whispering the words of the carols to herself.

'We're here,' announced Jinny. 'And Guizer's kicking up your trailer.'

'Probably pleased to hear you,' said Miss Tuke, trying on wings, and Mr Redding gave Jinny a pile of carol sheets, asking her to put one on every chair in the hall.

'But Shantih . . .' began Jinny.

'Stop fussing. Ken's with her,' said Miss Tuke and punted Jinny into the hall.

Already a few mothers who had brought their children were seated in the front rows, surrounded by handbags and shopping, reserving places for their friends. In front of them was the space for the angel choir and then the battered, wooden manger watched over by the donkey on wheels and the loblolly dog leaking its stuffing. Above the manger, hanging from the roof of the hall was a great star that Jinny hadn't seen before. It glittered with sequins and crystals, breathing rainbows as it swung round gently

Beyond the manger stood the double doors that would open to let in the kings.

As she laid out the carol sheets Jinny stared round the bare hall, hearing stray scraps of conversation about the weather, operations, food and families.

In the kitchen the costumed children were twittering with high excitement.

'Now you've not a thing to worry about,' Miss Broughton assured them. 'I'll be sitting at the end of the front row ready to prompt you. Not that anyone is going to forget, are you?'

The children giggled apprehensively, anxious to get the whole thing over, yet afraid to start.

'Remember, Mary and Joseph, Jesus is in the manger. When you reach him fold back the blanket so that the shepherds and Kings can see him.'

'Into our glad rags then,' said Miss Tuke and she went out with Jinny to where Ken was talking to Amanda Bowen who was dressed as an Arab.

'Jolly well done,' enthused Miss Tuke regarding Amanda's draperies with an approving eye.

'Thought as a royal horse holder I should be kind of Arabian. Piers was at a fancy dress do as the Red Shadow, so actually that's what I am,' and Amanda surveyed her robes with smooth self-satisfaction.

'Smug,' thought Jinny, but when Amanda took Shantih and Bramble with competent ease, Jinny accepted her.

In the kitchen Ken, Miss Tuke and Jinny put on their tunics and cloaks. Miss Broughton secured their crowns for them with hair clips.

'Magnificent,' said Mr Redding. 'A transformation. I trust you will be donating the costumes for all future kings?'

Jinny started to explain that he could have everything

except her mother's cloak but the hall was almost full. They were about to begin.

Through the kitchen door Mr Redding signalled to Miss Osborne at the piano, who lifted her outspread hands over the keyboard and crashed them down in the first notes of her Christmas medley. The audience shuffled, coughed and hushed each other expectantly. The angels, lined up two by two, waited for the parachute jump into the hall.

'Remember everyone, speak UP. Sing UP.'

The piano music stopped. Mr Redding's opening words were few.

'Now,' breathed Miss Broughton and the first pair of angels walked into the hall which darkened as they advanced, until only the lights above the manger were left on.

'Need to look smartish,' said Miss Tuke and she went stomping down to the field to take Guizer out of his trailer.

Jinny tightened her girths and mounted. Shantih humped her back in token bucks, springing stiff-legged as a racehorse as Jinny calmed her, whispering reassurance, clapping her neck.

Ken sat easily on Bramble, the austere silver crown seeming to grow from his head as if it were part of him. The stuff of Granny Mander's ball gown hung from his shoulders like dusty shadows and his kingfisher tunic glinted through the black branches of Jinny's painted tree.

Miss Tuke rode Guizer up from the field to where Ken and Jinny waited for her by the church gate, just beyond the glare of the spotlights. Guizer was a heavy, fifteen hand, dun Highland with an eel stripe and black haystack mane and tail. Miss Tuke's green wellies were thrust into her stirrups, her stubby legs in their red cords were slabbed against the saddle and the ruffles of her silver cloak were draped over Guizer's solid quarters.

'He's wondering what new madness we're up to now,' confided Miss Tuke, her short-fingered hand buried in Guizer's hearth rug shoulder.

'It's now,' thought Jinny. 'Now it's happening.'

Amanda Bowen who was watching through a small window at the side of the doors came running down the path in a swirl of Red Shadow robes to tell them that the shepherds had set off for Bethlehem.

'One of them spotted his mother and ran straight to her and another left his lamb behind and had to dash back for it,' she told them, giggling.

Icy water trickled down Jinny's spine, for how could she think it funny? How could she laugh at it?

The singing of "The First Nowell" came from the hall and Amanda, wishing them good luck, swirled her way back to the window and stood looking in.

Jinny waited, her eyes fixed on the wooden doors for the first vibration of their opening. They must be wide open before she galloped up to them. Not walk, the way Miss Tuke wanted, but gallop, the way the kings would have galloped at the end of their long searching.

There was a sudden sough of winter wind that blew down from the moor, from the red deer, from the white stag. Jinny saw the wind lift Ken's cloak and she remembered a moment from a film she had seen where men on horseback had ridden along the skyline, their cloaks billowing about them.

Amanda raised her hand and turning waved to them. Holding her breath Jinny stared at the doors, felt the crack between them tremble, saw a slit of light and then the manger, Joseph and Mary, the kneeling shepherds and the winged angels ranked on either side. Easing her fingers a fraction on the reins she let Shantih prance forward so that all the kings could be seen from the hall, then she waited.

'Get on girl!' ordered Miss Tuke but Jinny held Shantih between her hands and seat. Her legs niggled her on, her hands held her back, so that she could feel Shantih's energy, desperate as a caged bird to escape, to gallop to the manger, a horse of fire for the King of Gold.

'We three kings of orient are
Bearing gifts we traverse so far.
Field and fountain, moor and mountain
Following yonder star.'

Audience and angels craned forward at the sight of the kings, their gasps of amazement loud into the night.

'O star of wonder, star of night
Star of royal beauty bright.'

They sang the chorus while Amanda waved desperately and Jinny, staring at the dazzling of the star above the manger held Miss Tuke and Ken penned behind her. Not to show off, not only to make Shantih look wild and heraldic but because this was the way it had to be.

It was not until the last two lines of the chorus –

Westward leading, still proceeding
Guide us to thy perfect light.'

that Jinny sent Shantih galloping forward. In a frenzy of flying mane and plunging hooves the Arab went blazing through the spotlights. At the last possible second Jinny pulled her to a rearing halt. With both hands on the pommel of her saddle Jinny sprang upwards, twisting in mid air so that her cloak billowed about her as she dropped to the ground at Shantih's shoulder.

As if they had practised it a million times Amanda had given the golden gift to Jinny and had Shantih controlled by her bit ring.

Slowly, holding the box in both hands, Jinny walked to the manger, acknowledged Mary and Joseph, set down her gift and knelt to the Child.

'Is it that Manders lassie from Finmory?' asked a voice from the darkened hall.

'Aye, it is and that terrible wild horse she has.'

Jinny stood up, stepped back and took Shantih from Amanda, leading her to the side of the doorway so that Miss Tuke could ride Bramble to the centre.

Despite her mother's cloak it was not the Golden King they had seen, only the lass from Finmory. Disillusionment washed like a cold flood over Jinny's heart. They would not remember the play as the best ever nativity play, only as the play in which the Finmory lass had ridden up to the manger on her wild horse.

They sang the next chorus while Miss Tuke prepared to dismount. She kicked her feet free from the stirrups, took her reins in her left hand. Amanda stood ready with her gift. As Miss Tuke scrambled her leg over the saddle, Bramble snapped his teeth at Guizer's rump and the pony leapt sideways. Miss Tuke's welly caught in the cantle of her saddle, pitching her forward over Guizer's shoulder.

Somehow her cloak held her there and for a long moment she hung down with her arms stretched towards the ground, her crown askew and her green wellies pointing skywards, then there was the sound of tearing material and Miss Tuke was gently deposited onto the ground.

The singing had almost stopped as the audience watched Miss Tuke's slow descent but once they saw her safely on her feet again, their relief spread into grins, laughter bubbled up and was swallowed down, while Miss

Broughton quelled her giggling schoolchildren with a threatening forefinger.

'Frankincense to offer have I,' sang Mr Redding his voice rallying the audience who were wandering about, lost in the chorus.

With torn cloak, crown slipping from the back of her head Miss Tuke nodded in the direction of the manger, dumped down the silver box and hastily backed off, taking Guizer from Amanda.

'I hold you directly responsible for this whole thing, my girl,' she stated as she led Guizer across towards Shantih. 'Letting that horse behave like a lunatic.'

But Jinny was too lost in misery for Miss Tuke's words to reach her. The nativity play had been ruined. From far away Jinny thought she heard the roar of a stag but it was too distant for her to be certain. Maybe it was only her own misery that summoned it from the silent moors.

Ken dismounted, gave Bramble's reins to Amanda and stood, a straight, silent figure commanding the hall's attention, before he strode to the manger and going down on one knee set his black gift beside the others. He waited, his arms spread out, the shadow of the future crucifixion, and when he stood up again the audience had forgotten Miss Tuke's comedy turn.

They sang 'What shall I give him,' while children too young to be in the play came up to the manger and gave toys, books and games and suddenly it was over Everyone was standing singing 'O Come All Ye Faithful'. Jinny listened to the carol, too miserable to join in. Mr Redding thanked everyone for coming and directed them into the church for the watchnight service. Children ran to their parents. A little girl reclaimed her donkey. Miss Broughton gathered in costumes. Mr Redding hoped Miss Tuke hadn't hurt herself.

'Enjoyed it so much,' congratulated Mrs Manders. 'You looked really stunning Jinny, though I did think for one horrible moment that you were going to come charging into the hall.'

'I didn't expect you to think anything else,' said Jinny desolate, but already her mother was commiserating with Miss Tuke and saying how sweet the little ones looked.

Mrs Manders took her cloak which seemed now no more that a rather old fashioned evening cloak. Miss Broughton took the crowns saying they could let her have the rest of their costumes later. Gradually the hall emptied. Miss Tuke took Guizer back to his trailer and went into church with Mr Manders.

'What are you two doing?' Mrs Manders asked Ken and Jinny, giving Jinny her duffle coat and hard hat which she had collected from the hall.

'Going home,' said Jinny bleakly.

'We're popping into church,' said Mrs Manders deciding it best to pay no attention to Jinny's mood. 'Don't hang around. Too cold.'

The hall doors were closed. A last mother holding her four year old son firmly by the hand hurried home. She stopped for a moment beside Shantih.

'Now I am telling you for the last time, the horse did not have wings. Be seeing for yourself.'

The little boy stared up at Shantih, his eyes wide with tiredness and excitement.

'I saw them,' he stated stubbornly. 'It was the golden wings it had.'

'You're right,' said Ken, speaking directly to the little boy. 'I saw them too.'

'Filling his head with such nonsense,' snapped the woman but the child's face lit up as he smiled at Ken.

'You see,' said Ken as they watched the little boy being dragged away. 'It is always worthwhile. All his life he'll remember Shantih's golden wings. Tell his grandchildren about them.'

A surge of gratitude lifted through Jinny. It had all been worthwhile – the hassle, the striving, the not giving in. For the little boy the nativity play had been as wonderful as Jinny had wanted it to be for everyone.

'That's the way it is,' said Ken. 'No one to hand out bouquets. Most of the time you don't know anyone has heard you. But nice when you do. A true gift.'

'A true gift,' Jinny repeated to herself and at once she remembered the photgraph in her pocket. Without giving herself time to think up reasons why she shouldn't, she took it out, spread it open over Shantih's withers and forced herself to look at it.

The heap of dead deer piled casually on top of each other, soft sculptures of their living beings. This was how it was – both more and less. More than the routine, unseen, accepted slaughter of the creatures that was so unecessary, so pathetic. The dead deer deserved Jinny's engulfing sadness, at such destruction. But it was less than the phantasmagoric dance of Jinny's lurid fear. The nostril dripping blood was no more than that; the glazed eyes did not open "in a lane to the land of the dead". Defused, accepted, the photograph had lost its power of terror. Having looked at it Jinny was freed from it.

Slowly Jinny looked away and her glance caught the headline DEER POACHERS STRIKE AGAIN.

"Deer poachers in the north east of Scotland are playing havoc with herds of red deer," read the article. "The deer are herded together, shot down and their carcases taken south where hoteliers are willing to pay Christmas prices to add offerings from Santa's team to their menus. The red deer pictured below were found in a siding off country road in Banchor. It is thought that the poachers were about to load this little lot when they were disturbed

104

by a police patrol car. The gang, whoever they may be, are no amateurs and so far the police have been unable to track them down. It is estimated that some two hundred deer may have been taken, which means more than pennies in the poachers' pockets."

As Jinny's eyes darted over the print the pieces of the jigsaw, like a film run backwards, clicked into place – the helicopter driving the deer together on the Ardtallon moors, the men with their geologist cover story giving them the unchallenged freedom of the moors, their voices overheard when she had been sheltering in the croft doorway, 'Christmas Eve. One o'clock for the drop. Over the border by three,' the geologist driving the huge removal van into which they would load the dead deer.

It was tonight they were planning to take the deer. The drop was the sheer drop from the Ardtallon moors to the road.

Jinny thrust the paper at Ken.

'The geologists are poachers,' she cried, her tongue tripping over the words. 'That's why all the deer are at Ardtallon. They've been collecting them there with that helicopter. I overheard them planning it. Tonight. One o'clock they're going to kill them. Load them into their van on the Ardtallon road.'

'We've got to get help,' said Ken, instantly understanding. 'Can't stop them ourselves. Phone the police.'

They galloped down the road to the phone box outside the garage. Jinny flung herself off Shantih, thrust her reins at Ken and dashed into the phone box.

'Please God, let it be working,' she prayed as she grabbed up the receiver. 'Please God,' and it was.

She thrust ten pence into the slot, dialled the number for Ardtallon Police Station and waited with her finger on the coin, ready to push it in the second the tone changed.

But the phone rang out again and again. Jinny's urgent hope set cold inside her as the phone rang on and no one answered it.

There was no one at the police station. If you got no reply you were meant to phone the Inverburgh police station but what use would that be? By the time Jinny had convinced the Inverburgh police that her story was true and they had driven out to Ardtallon the deer would be dead. The white stag dead.

Despairing, Jinny banged down the receiver and snatched it up again. She phoned Finmory and Mike answered at once.

'It's Jinny,' she said. 'Listen,' she garbled out her story. 'You've got to keep on phoning the police at Ardtallon. The geologists' van will be parked somewhere by the rocks where they go up sheer from the road. They must get there before one o'clock or they'll be too late.'

'I'll try,' said Mike accepting Jinny's story without question and Jinny flung down the receiver and dashed back to Ken.

'Can't get the police,' she shouted as she threw herself onto Shantih. 'Mike's going to keep on trying. *We've* got to get to Ardtallon. *We've* got to save the deer.'

'The road?' asked Ken.

'No use,' said Jinny. 'Never get up the rocks, they'd see us. We've got to ride over the moors. If we can reach them in time there must be some way we can stop them.'

Jinny swung Shantih round and with a rearing plunge Shantih was galloping out of Glenbost, Bramble thundering beside her.

When they reached the track that left the Finmory road to cross the moors towards Ardtallon it was almost midnight. They had an hour in which to find the poachers.

'Not long enough,' thought Jinny desperately. By daylight they would have had a chance but not in this light, when moon shadows cast pits of darkness in their way and the moors were a weird, unknown landscape, all familiar landmarks changed and where the frozen ground set snares at every galloping stride.

Jinny thrust the memory of Shantih's fall from her mind. She had to reach Ardtallon in time. Last night she had failed the Red Horse, failed Sara. This was the last chance to save the deer.

Jinny crouched low over Shantih's withers, drummed her on to greater speed. She thought she heard Ken shouting to her to go on as Bramble's hoofbeats fell away behind her and Jinny was alone. Only herself to reach the deer, to find some way of saving them.

'One o'clock for the drop,' and only herself to stop the poachers from slaughtering them.

CHAPTER TWELVE

A sudden flurry of snow came blowing across the moors as Jinny reached the end of the sheep track she had been following. She brought Shantih to a halt, stood up in her stirrups, staring frantically about, searching for any landmark, but she could see nothing she recognized. It was a quarter past twelve and every moment she wasted gave her less time to reach the deer.

Even if she had been galloping over the Finmory moors that she knew almost as well as their own garden, Jinny would have found it difficult to know where she was going but now on the Ardtallon moors she could do no more than ride in the general direction of Ardtallon.

Jinny was still sure that it lay ahead of her. She gathered Shantih together and sent her on over the heather. Now she had no track to follow she couldn't risk galloping, had to hold Shantih to a steady trot but even at that speed Shantih tripped and stumbled over the blind, treacherous going.

The snow was falling more steadily, settling on walls and in the crevices of boulders. Its white powder dusted bracken and heather and frosted Shantih's mane.

'I'm being too slow,' thought Jinny desperately. 'Far too slow. I've got to reach them. Got to save them somehow. If I had ridden out onto the moor last night I could have done something to save them. I know I could. Then there would have been time.'

The nativity play was behind her now, its urgency vanished. It seemed no more than a trifle of snowflake and tinsel.

'I should have known that I had to go when Sara called me,' Jinny told herself, over and over again as she forced Shantih on. 'Shouldn't have let my father stop me.'

Jinny jumped three walls in quick succession, holding her breath each time in case there should be scattered stones on the landing side. They reached a flat stretch of moorland and Jinny urged Shantih into a gallop, only pulling her back when the heather became littered with scattered boulders, some the height of Shantih's knees.

It was half past twelve. The hush of falling snow was all about them. Catching her foot from a walk, Shantih almost came down but somehow found her balance again. Terrified in case Shantih fell, Jinny tugged on her reins, jerking Shantih to a halt. Looking round she was suddenly no longer sure of her way, no longer certain that Ardtallon lay ahead, thought she had come too far or climbed too high.

Jinny turned Shantih back the way they had come, took a few strides, then uncertainly half turned and rode in that direction, only to stop again. The snow closed her into a paperweight world. Half an hour ago the moors had stretched about her in a moon-blanched distance. The mountains had risen crystalline against the sky but now Jinny could see nothing except the falling snow. With a sickening clutch of fear she knew that she was lost, totally and completely lost. She would never reach the deer now, never save the white stag. The curtains of snow closed in and the panic of her wanderings in the snow blizzard when she had nearly frozen to death searching for Shantih, filled Jinny's mind. There was nothing she could do except sit paralysed by fear.

Suddenly Shantih, who had been standing with her quarters against the snow, plunged round whinnying and raced forward at a high – stepping trot. She stopped, whinnied again and from somewhere ahead came the bellow of a stag. As surely as if she galloped across grass, Shantih raced towards the sound.

Ahead of them something moved. White, even in the falling snow, the stag bounded in front of them and, whinnying, Shantih followed. Jinny was no more than a helpless passenger on her back. Each time Shantih almost caught up with the stag it would bound forward and Shantih would follow it, no longer tripping or hesitating, but cantering freely on.

Gradually the snow stopped, the moon rode high in a cloudless sky again and as Shantih galloped on Jinny gazed over a bright expanse of hills patched with snow, all her senses alert for any sign of deer or poachers.

Suddenly Shantih stopped. The white stag had vanished into the camouflage of snow and Jinny was alone. She stood up in her stirrups, staring around. For seconds she could see nothing and then Shantih walked forward and Jinny was looking down into a natural trap formed by the sheer rock fall down to the Ardtallon road and rocks rising up on two sides. Trapped between the rocks and the drop, some twenty or thirty deer milled in a panic of constant movement. Between the jaws of the rock there was a narrow opening and for a mad moment Jinny could not think why the deer didn't race through it to freedom, couldn't see why they stayed in this trap.

Then something moved in the gap. Moonlight sparkled on metal. A man moved out of the shadows to stand dark against the snow. It was the Smiler geologist and in the crook of his arm Jinny saw to her horror he was carrying a rifle. For a paralysed moment Jinny stared down at him, knowing that he had only to look up and he would see her.

She heard his voice, another man's voice answering and knew that there were two of the poachers guarding the gap.

A stag broke from the trapped herd, charged towards

110

the gap and in an instant a bullet screamed high over the head of the stag, turning it back into the panicking mass of deer.

Taking advantage of the diversion, Jinny swung Shantih round and rode her swiftly out of sight. When she was certain the poachers couldn't see her she halted Shantih who stood head alert, gazing in the direction of the deer.

Held in a clutch of terror, Jinny had no idea what to do. The white stag had led her here and now it seemed that there was nothing she could do except wait to hear the rifle shots as the poachers destroyed the deer.

Jinny recognized the place where the deer were trapped. It was where she had picnicked with Dolina, where the almost vertical track led up from the road.

'If only Ken hadn't been left behind. He would have known what to do,' Jinny thought wildly. If she had ridden out last night Jinny was sure the white stag would have led Shantih to the deer. Then she would have had hours in which to find a way of saving them. But now there was hardly any time left. In minutes it would be one o'clock.

'They can't. They can't,' Jinny muttered through clenched teeth. 'I can't sit here and let them kill the deer!'

Could she ride Shantih through the herd, forcing them to break out through the gap to freedom? Could she? Would the poachers be desperate enough to shoot at Shantih? Would the deer pass the poachers' guns?

Suddenly she heard a sound a little way behind her. Not a noise that was part of the moors at night, but a definite, spine chilling sound. The sound of a poacher who had spotted her watching from the hillside above?

Jinny twisted sharply round in her saddle. A dark shape was standing a few steps away from her but it wasn't a poacher, it was Tam.

'We couldn't find this place without you,' he muttered accusingly. 'Why did you not come when Sara called you?

111

Your horse would have been fast enough to have followed the stag.'

'Dad wouldn't . . .' began Jinny but Tam paid no attention to her.

'I couldn't find them until tonight. Those two men with the guns have got them trapped.'

'They're poachers,' whispered Jinny. 'They're going to shoot the deer at one o'clock. They've got a van waiting on the road below. Going to load the dead deer into the van and sell them down south as venison. If only we could find some way to drive the deer out onto the moors but there's no way. They're all going to be killed.'

'There is,' said Tam. 'Fire. Fire will drive them through the gap. I'm going to get a branch burning and chase them with it.'

'A branch!' scorned Jinny. 'Set fire to a branch, just like that?'

Tam scuttled back and lifted a branch from the heather where he had dropped it. It was tied with strips of sacking and as he moved it Jinny smelt the pungent stink of paraffin.

'After I found the deer I went down to a farm. Made this in a barn. This'll burn. The fire will drive them past the men,' said Tam, rattling a box of matches in his jacket pocket. 'I've got to get round between the deer and the drop.'

'The poachers will hear you,' warned Jinny but Tam was away.

'Can't sit here doing nothing,' Jinny thought desperately and squeezing her legs against Shantih's sides she urged her forward until she could look down on the huddled deer again.

Suddenly she saw the white stag standing on the moor beyond the poachers. She felt Shantih's urgent, prick-eared attention as she too saw the stag. Then with a

112

flurry of her nostrils, as if in answer to the stag, Shantih plunged forward, straight down to the poachers.

Her knuckles pressed against Shantih's neck, her knees digging into the saddle, Jinny was carried helplessly along. As Shantih plunged on, Jinny felt a worm of fear twist in her stomach. The poachers had guns. The deer they were going to kill would be worth hundreds of pounds to them. They were not going to let Jinny and Tam stop them without a fight. If they should shoot Shantih. . .

Then Jinny felt the sword of the Golden King hanging at her side and she remembered how sharp and pointed its blade was. The Golden King would be equal to any poacher. As Shantih galloped on, Jinny straightened her back and sat tall in the saddle.

A rank stench rose from the deer as they milled about in the enclosed space, close packed, on the brink of total panic. Stags and hinds were mixed together, their quicksilver eyes moon glazed, their nostrils and rabbit lips twitching with fear, the fans of their ears tense and trembling.

All vitally alive, all dead, if Tam did not succeed in driving them through the gap in the rock trap.

'But he must! He must!' screamed Jinny silently. She could not bear to think that the deer were about to be killed.

'What the devil are you doing here?' yelled one of the poachers, turning the smiling mask of his face at Jinny as she reached the gap. 'Get the blazes out of here.'

'Let the deer go,' challenged Jinny but her words were drowned by the white stag's bellowing roar as it came charging past the men. It battled its way through the herd and racing up and down between the deer and the rock's edge it tried to force the deer out past the poachers.

Shantih screamed with a sound that Jinny had never heard her make before. Without any urging from Jinny she was galloping, neck outstretched, head low as a stallion's, straight at the poacher with the smiling face. She reared up in front of him and before the man had a chance to take aim Shantih drove down with her forefeet and catching him on the shoulder, sent him crashing to the ground. Clinging, terrified, to Shantih's mane Jinny hardly knew whether she rode her own Arab or sat astride the fury of the Red Horse.

From the corner of her eye she saw flames blossom on the branches held by a manic figure that danced at the rock's edge. For the first time since she had seen the trapped deer Jinny thought they had a chance of saving them, for surely the fire would drive them out to the freedom of the moors. She thought for a second that some of the deer had broken past the poachers, thought, with lifting hope, that if some broke free the rest would follow, that there was a chance.

In the same instant she knew that they had failed. With blank dismay she knew there was nothing more they could do to stop the deer being killed, for the poachers were not planning to shoot the deer and throw their bodies over the cliff. Through the night came the droning, rumble of an approaching helicopter, the helicopter that would drive the deer to their death.

The slit-mouthed poacher fired at the deer, turning them. The other poacher was back on his feet, reaching for his rifle.

But there was no urgency now. The deer had heard the helicopter. They stood rigid at its approach, as it came in over the moors straight towards them. It would swoop in low over them, driving them over the rock. Between the deer and the rock's edge stood Tam, still waving his glowing, burnt-out branch.

The realization scorched through Jinny that Tam too would be killed for he could never stand against the surging terror of the deer. He would be swept over the cliff with them.

Without thought, Jinny drove Shantih past the poachers, rode her close to the rocks, screaming to Tam that he must get back from the edge or he would be killed.

Realizing the danger he was in, Tam dropped the branches and ran full tilt to Shantih.

'Jump up,' Jinny yelled. 'Spring up behind me.'

She felt Tam's hands gripping her waist, felt him squirm and fight his way onto Shantih and the helicopter was upon them. Seat driving into the saddle, heels hard against Shantih's sides, Jinny fought with every fibre of her being to force Shantih forward into the path of the oncoming nightmare of the helicopter, fought to hold her steady against the brutal stampede of the deer.

'Go on! Don't turn round! GO ON! GO ON!' Jinny screamed at her horse. 'Shantih go forward. Get on!' Her words were a frenzied jumble of terror.

Jinny kept Shantih against the rocks on one side while on her other side were the stampeding deer, their eyes enormous with terror and their tongues flagging from their mouths. In the press they lunged and fell, rising above each other like waves in a tumultuous sea until they hurtled over the edge of the rock.

The helicopter was almost above them, sweat ran down Shantih's neck and shoulders as Jinny fought to hold her against the death charge. As the helicopter roared over them Shantih shook violently, then stood stock still as it rumbled on over the Ardtallon road.

The few deer who had escaped spun round and raced to the hills and the poachers, ignoring Jinny, raced to the edge of the cliff, hauled up some sort of gate or barricade of barbed wire Jinny had't noticed before and disappeared down the track to the road.

Tam jumped to the ground and Jinny slid down from

Shantih and was very sick. She clung to Shantih wiping her face on her sleeve shuddering uncontrollably.

'If I had come last night,' she mouthed.

'Aye,' said Tam.

A million times worse than the photograph was the thought of the dead deer lying at the foot of the cliff. It was the photograph made hideously real.

'This is not the way things happen,' thought Jinny wildly. 'I should have found some way to save them. At the last minute I should have found a way to let them escape.'

On the road below the poachers would be dragging the warm carcases into their van. They would drive south with them. Sell them to hotels for a handsome profit. It was not right that they should be allowed to make money from their cruel destruction.

For a long moment Jinny stood, still leaning against Shantih. She had not been able to stop the poachers killing the deer but she knew how she could stop them driving the carcases away. Knew how she could do it, if she had the courage.

Jinny squared her shoulders, forcing herself to go on when all she wanted to do was to bury her face in Shantih's mane and cry her heart out.

'We're going down the track after them,' she told Tam. 'Dolina said Callum went down it, so we can go too. I'm going to stop them selling the deer.'

Jinny marched Shantih to the edge of the rock. Her legs were liquid at the thought of scrambling down the almost vertical track. Jinny had no head for heights and she remembered vividly how the loose chippings of rock had slipped away from under her feet when she had led Shantih up onto the moors for their picnic. Now there would be the giddy drop beneath her.

She looked over the rock edge and saw the track as little

116

more than a scratching on the vertical fall of rock. She could see where the poachers had fixed the barbed wire barrier to stop the deer getting down the track and below this there seemed to Jinny nothing but a sheer fall to the road below. She could not, could not make herself go down it.

Tam led the way. Neat-footed he crept silently down.

'Now,' Jinny told herself. 'Step out now,' and she forced herself to take the first step onto the track.

Gritting her teeth, digging her nails into the palms of her hands, her mouth brick dry, she made her feet inch downward, when left to themselves they would have rooted, held her to the spot, unable to move forward or back. As Jinny crept down she made a small creaking noise in the back of her throat, an animal sound of terror.

Somewhere behind her Jinny was aware of Shantih making her own way down. Her iron shod hooves slipped and slid on the loose rock shale. She moved with her front legs splayed, her quarters crouched down.

The track twisted away from where the powerful headlights of the poachers' van were beamed on the deer. Their blinding glare made darkness of the moonlight, shielding Tam, Jinny and Shantih from the poachers' sight as they shot the deer that were still alive and dragged the carcases from the bottom of the rock face to pile them by the removal van, ready to load them.

About half way down there was a gap in the track. It was just too wide for Jinny to stride across it. She would have to jump. She saw Tam leap nimbly over, hardly aware that it was there and then the gulf yawned in front of her. She knew that she could not cross it, could not possibly force herself to jump over it.

Pressing her back against the wall of the rock face Jinny stretched out one leg but she could hardly reach half way

117

across. She drew her foot back, digging her fingernails into the rock behind her. She could feel the space beneath her pulling her down, dragging her off the track.

'MUST,' Jinny commanded herself. 'Must go on. You've got to get down. Can't let them get away.'

But the soles of her feet clutched at the track beneath her, gripped her there. She could not move the least centimetre.

'Stay back,' she muttered, hearing Shantih close behind her. 'You can't pass me.'

Then she felt Shantih's bulk pushing against her. Jinny screwed her eyes tight shut, was certain she was about to fall through space, Shantih and herself crashing into the ground below.

Jinny stuffed her knuckled fist into her mouth, bit down hard on it and forced herself to open her eyes again. She was looking straight at Shantih's quarters.

Without giving herself time to think, Jinny reached her arm over Shantih's back and grasping her withers she leapt across the gap and landed safely clutching Shantih's mane.

'What's wrong?' demanded Tam, coming back to see what was stopping Jinny.

'Nothing,' Jinny lied, hardly able to speak. 'It's okay,' and she crept on, inch by agonizing inch.

At last they reached the ground and Jinny stood shaking, relief flooding over her. The ground solid, secure beneath her feet.

'Hold Shantih,' Jinny whispered urgently, thrusting Shantih's reins at Tam. Having survived the climb down the rock nothing could stop her. She knew exactly what she was going to do.

The poachers had finished shooting the deer and were lugging the carcases to the back of the van. Jinny watched, waited until all three poachers had their backs turned to

118

her, then she dashed silently forward and crouched at the front of the van.

Holding her breath, she drew the Golden King's sword from its scabbard, and lifting it above her head, plunged it into the front tyre. The wall of the tyre was stronger than Jinny had expected and it took the full force of her body to jab the blade in.

The explosion of air screamed into the night. The bulk of the van shuddered and settled as Jinny wrenched the sword free and drove it into the other front tyre.

The Smiler reached Jinny first. Swearing, he grabbed her by the shoulder and flung her against the side of the van.

'What the devil are you at now?' he yelled. 'Blasted kid. I told you to get the blazes out of this.'

'You killed the deer! You destroyed them!' Jinny cried, tears of rage and exhaustion running down her face. 'But you're not going to get them away from here. You'll have to leave them. You're too late. If you stay you'll be discovered. The police will be here. My brother's telling them.'

The man hit out at Jinny, catching her across the head and knocking her to the ground. As she fell the night erupted with noise – the blare of police sirens, the scream of brakes, car doors being thrust open and policemen bursting into the night.

'It's the cops! Run for it,' yelled the Smiler as he spun round in a dash for freedom. Jinny flung herself at him, grabbed his ankle and sent him sprawling to the ground. In an instant a policeman had captured him.

But the tadpole man stood without moving.

'Good evening officer,' he said, his face showing no emotion as he held out his wrist to be handcuffed. 'Isn't it rather late for a nice boy like yourself to be wandering about?'

The third poacher who had been furthest from the van ran headlong into the darkness and seemed to have escaped until Tam's voice, screeching loud as a night bird, screamed to tell them where he was and two of the policemen caught him.

There was a clatter of hooves on the road and as the two policemen brought back the slit-mouthed poacher Ken came riding up.

'Have they got them?' he demanded as he jumped to the ground. 'Were they in time?'

'Not in time to save the deer,' Jinny said, her lower lip trembling, her voice gulping, so that she could hardly speak.

Ken put his arm round her, drawing her to him, comforting her where there could be no comfort, for the grace and beauty of the deer were now no more than a broken, bloody heap of dead bodies.

'If I'd come last night . . .' Jinny began as a policeman came over to them.

'A good night's work,' he said. 'We've been after this lot for a few months now. Nearly had them at Banchor but they gave us the slip. It would be your brother who phoned us? Finmory House?'

Scrubbing her knuckles into her eyes Jinny said, yes it would be Mike, that he'd promised to keep on phoning Ardtallon Police Station.

'Had the sense to phone us at Inverburgh and we got on the move at once. Still, mustn't keep you here. We'll be round at Finmory tomorrow to get some details from you. Been a disturbing business for you. Least you know that you've helped to stop them. They'll not be after deer again, I can promise you that.'

Jinny nodded desolately. Now it was over she only wanted to be home again.

'Could we drive you back?'

'We've got the horses,' said Jinny.

'Sure you can manage?'

Ken said they could and Jinny nodded, longing and longing to be home.

'Don't waste any more time then,' said the policeman. 'We'll phone your family to let them know you're on your way.'

'Got to get home,' Jinny muttered wearily, going to take Shantih from Tam, but Tam's bony hand gripped Shantih's reins.

'You can't,' he stated. 'You must come to the ceremony. Must bring your red horse.'

Jinny stared blankly at Tam, slowly remembering the tinkers' Christmas ceremony and how Sara had told her to be there. She knew that if her parents could see her, she would be sent home in a police car and Ken would bring Shantih and Bramble home. More than anything Jinny longed to be safe in bed, to sleep, to blot out the night's horror. But she knew that she had no choice. If her father had not stopped her obeying Sara's summons last night the deer might still have been alive. This time she must obey Sara.

'I must go,' she said to Ken who had waited without speaking, until Jinny had made up her own mind.

'Right,' said Ken, tightening Bramble's girths and mounting.

'I know the place,' said Tam. 'Along the road and then onto the moor again.'

Before Jinny rode away she made herself look at the dead deer. She was almost sure that one of the broken carcases was white.

CHAPTER THIRTEEN

When they went back onto the moors Tam walked at Shantih's head. Jinny was so tired that she only wanted to sleep. Deep sleep without dreams; to blot out the stampeding deer, the helicopter's roar and the moments when she had felt that she had not enough strength to hold Shantih against the panic of the deer and they must carry Tam, Shantih and herself over the rock to certain death.

The day had gone on forever – centuries since she had been shopping in Inverburgh, fighting with Petra. Even the nativity play seemed to have taken place long ago. Yet it had all been today – but Jinny checked herself. It had all happened yesterday. Today it was Christmas Day.

Tam led them through an enchanted landscape. The moonlight glittered on the snow-diamonded moors and it seemed to Jinny that the air they breathed was bright with moon rainbows, that the violence of the red deer's destruction had flipped into its opposite and she rode through a world of peace and contentment, for yet again the Christ Child had been born, the world renewed.

A small group of tinkers were waiting for them. At first Jinny had thought they were boulders, a part of the moors, for they were so still. Then she made out Sara and saw there were three other women, a young girl carrying a baby warmly wrapped against the cold, and two men – one young, one older than Sara. The older man carried a heavy, richly bound Bible, the younger one a tattered bag.

Sara lifted her arm in greeting. She came straight to Jinny and rested her hand on Jinny's.

'Forgive yourself,' she said. 'The lesson has been learnt.'

You come with us tonight where many would have turned away.'

Jinny looked down at her. Felt her peace and healing, her understanding.

'But the deer?' she pleaded.

'What deer?' replied Sara.

Jinny did not know what she meant, for Tam had rushed ahead telling Sara that the deer had been destroyed. Of course Sara knew what deer. Jinny wanted to shout back at her for the stupidity of her answer but she could not, for ridiculous as it sounded, it touched some sleeping corner of Jinny's mind, dawned with a truth that was just out of reach, where deer to earth, earth to plants, plants to animals and again animals to earth, moved in a circling dance of delight.

But Ken smiled. Understood.

They went on, Sara leading them now. All weariness had left Jinny. As they made their way through the silvered world she felt as if she flowed within a river, was carried along and had no need to struggle or grab, for everything here was hers and it had always been so. She had only dreamt it was otherwise.

They came to a hollow in the moor and Jinny recognized it as the place where she had first seen the white stag. On two sides were the falls of rock and scree, while infront of them, lifting in easy ledges, was a high rock. In the hollow it was as mild as a spring day. The moon shone directly into the hollow making the light more intense and when Jinny turned and looked out to the moor again, she could see the far brilliance of the sea.

The young man carrying the bag took a small, broken loaf of rough bread out of it and set it on a ledge of rock some four feet from the ground. Beside it he placed an earthenware pot of salt and pouring water from a bottle into a glass, he placed it next to the salt.

Sara lit a candle and set it to burn on a higher ledge. The praying hands of flame lifted into the night. The young woman with the baby sat down on a boulder at the side of the rock. Sara stood opposite the young woman, the candle burning between them. Every movement the tinkers made was simple and direct.

Jinny, Ken, Tam, the young man and the two other tinker women took their places in a half circle around the candle. The old man stood in the centre of the circle and opening the Bible he held it before him, the palms of his hands flat against its covers. He waited a moment and the silence was absolute. Then he read in a rasping, gravel voice theprophecy of the coming of Christ from the book of Isiah.

'For unto us a child is born
Unto us a son is given
And the government shall be upon his shoulder
And his name shall be called
Wonderful
Counsellor
The mighty God
The everlasting Father
The Prince of Peace.'

He read it first facing the lighted candle and the baby, then to the three other quarters of the circle. When he had finished he placed the open Bible on the ground in front of the candle and took his place in the circle.

Here there were no costumes, no kings, no one striving to make this simple ceremony the best ever. It was as it was. Suddenly Jinny saw that all her efforts to turn the Glenbost nativity play into a spectacular happening had only been a way of showing off, wanting to make people see her as the best king, to admire Shantih. She hadn't

124

really cared about the nativity. She had only cared about Jinny Manders being the most.

They went one by one and knelt before the Child. Sara first, the other tinkers, then Ken, and last of all Jinny. It seemed they moved in a formal, precise dance in which all played their part – those who waited and those who knelt. Jinny would have left Shantih as Ken had left Bramble but Sara motioned her to take Shantih with her. While Jinny knelt Shantih breathed warm sweet breath over the baby, who opened his eyes and laughed.

As they waited in the silent circle the white stag stepped out onto a ledge high above them.

It had escaped from the slaughter, stood imperious and royal, its crown of antlers lifted up. The snow on the rock behind it did not take from the stag's brilliance for it burnt from its own centre. For a moment as Jinny looked up at it she saw the Child held within its antlers, saw it with a vision as burning as when she had seen the angels in the church hall.

In a little while the stag turned away and was gone. The old man lifted the Bible and closed it. The young man put away the water, salt and bread. Sara blew out the candle and the mother stood up holding her baby close to her. When they left the hollow there was nothing to show that they had been there.

The tinkers, Ken and Jinny stayed together until Finmory House came into sight. Then the tinkers climbed into the hills making for their bothy. Jinny and Ken mounted their horses and rode down to Finmory.

'Christmas,' said Jinny smiling at Ken, and for a moment she balanced the mystical white stag, and the Christ Child's birth with the thought of presents, mince pies and her family. She understood them both, for they were two sides of the same weaving, together making the wholeness of things in which even the destruction of the deer had its place.

'Christmas!' Jinny said again, beaming.

She would apologize to Petra for taking her shawl and try, really try, to stop fighting so much with her. Another gift for the Child – to really look at her relationship with her sister.

'I'll paint a picture of Shantih, the tinkers and the white stag cradling the Child in its antlers,' Jinny promised herself. 'So I won't forget how it was. Not ever.'

Knowing she was nearly home, Shantih flirted suddenly sideways, kicked her heels to the sky and in a maze of silken mane and tail pranced her way down to Finmory. Jinny laughed aloud with delight and, with Ken riding beside her, she cantered on to where a Finmory Christmas was waiting to be unwrapped.

THE SILVER BRUMBY SERIES

ELYNE MITCHELL

Brumbies are the wild horses of Australia, hunted by man to be tamed for his own use. These six stories tell of Thowra, the Silver Brumby, and Kunama, his daughter, Wirramirra, his son, and Baringa, his grandson.

'These Brumby books are in a class by themselves . . . the horselover's dream' *Noel Steatfeild*

SILVER BRUMBY
SILVER BRUMBY'S DAUGHTER
SILVER BRUMBIES OF THE SOUTH
SILVER BRUMBY KINGDOM
SILVER BRUMBY WHIRLWIND
SON OF THE WHIRLWIND

ARMADA